HORSE GIRL

BY CARRIE SEIM

ILLUSTRATIONS BY STEPH WALDO

PENGUIN WORKSHOP

For every horse person, young or old.
May you ride bravely through life exactly as you are.
May you gallop after your dreams, no matter how wild.
May your heart remain untamed.

—CS

PENGUIN WORKSHOP
An Imprint of Penguin Random House LLC, New York

Emoji (used throughout): calvindexter/DigitalVision Vectors/Getty Images

Text copyright © 2021 by Carrie Seim. Illustrations copyright © 2021 by Penguin Random House LLC. All rights reserved. Published by Penguin Workshop, an imprint of Penguin Random House LLC, New York. PENGUIN and PENGUIN WORKSHOP are trademarks of Penguin Books Ltd, and the W colophon is a registered trademark of Penguin Random House LLC. Printed in the USA.

Visit us online at www.penguinrandomhouse.com.

Library of Congress Control Number: 2020049505

ISBN 9780593095485   10 9 8 7 6 5 4 3 2 1

CHAPTER ONE

"Heads up! Center oxer!"

Amara's voice echoes through the indoor riding ring as she and Silver Streak—a gorgeous, leggy black jumper—canter toward a wooden fence in perfect rhythm. Even their glossy ponytails bounce at the exact same time. Which is completely annoying. And then *mesmerizing*. And then annoying for tricking me into being mesmerized. Ugh.

Amara is oh-so-politely warning everyone at Oakwood Riding Academy to get *out* of her way. Move it or lose it, breeches. She's basically QUEEN OF THE #HORSEGIRLS (as her T-shirt helpfully explains to anyone who wasn't clear on this point), so we all *click-click* at our steeds, who scatter like stable mice.

Or at least they're supposed to.

I, however, am perched on Clyde Lee—one of the oldest, giant-est, willful-est horses at Oakwood. Clyde is half

Clydesdale, half thoroughbred, and 100 percent not budging.

He and I got matched up because I'm what they call a "novice" rider, aka "inexperienced," aka "Peasant of the #HorseGirls." Clyde is massive—several hands higher than any other horse here—a sturdy bay with white feathers on three of his fetlocks and an ivory blaze down his muzzle, sort of like he got caught with his nose and three hooves in a jar of vanilla frosting.[1]

Which, um, I can relate.

Being half draft horse, he's what my grandmother would call "big boned"—Clyde wasn't bred for delicate dressage or breezy show jumping. His hooves are each the size of a medium pizza! But he works his heart out in the ring. And he's always down for a snack. In other words, we totally get each other.[2]

I'm not sure if I was built for my life, either. My name might as well be "Wow, You're Tall for a Girl." And let's face it—walking my Breyer model horses through the miniature jump course in my bedroom and wearing breeches to school might have been cute in fourth grade, but it makes me certifiably dork-tagious in seventh. (In my defense: 1. It's a

---

1   Fetlocks are joints on horses' legs just above their hooves. Some horses grow long, swishy "feathers" there—kind of like it's spirit day and they tied pom-poms to their ankles.

2   Draft horses are GINORMOUS and bred to pull sleds and other heavy stuff. They're not built for dressage (a fancy sport where riders guide horses through teeny, tiny, delicate dances) or show jumping. Imagine the Rock trying to perform a dainty ballet leap—that's basically me and Clyde.

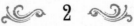 2

visualization exercise! 2. Breeches were invented way before yoga pants. You do your athleisure and I'll do mine.)[3]

I honestly don't care if everyone at school thinks I'm a horse-girl weirdo. I think anyone who *doesn't* love horses is a weirdo. Ponies are my passion, and I am leaning in.

Unfortunately, Clyde is only mine on lesson days. My family can't afford our own horse, unlike most of the girls at Oakwood, who were practically born in a tack room. So we have to make the most of our time together.

Clyde Lee may be "just" a stable horse, but that "just" is the single best thing to happen in my entire life. On the day of my riding lessons, I run (gallop) home from school and fly up to my room as fast as my clumsy feet can go.

I usually throw on my favorite practice shirt—BARN HAIR, DON'T CARE—over the aforementioned breeches, which I've had on since approximately 7:00 a.m. I braid my frizzy waves into two tight halos, tug on my boots, and snap on my velvet helmet. Ta-da, I'm ready!

Roughly two hours before my lesson.

"Nice crash helmet, Wills!" My dad finds this joke equally funny every time he says it. He thinks my turnout—the fancy word for gear worn by #HorseGirls and their steeds—is hilarious. I find his cargo shorts and dad sneakers similarly hilarious.

---

3   Who needs yoga pants? Breeches are stretchy pants with suede patches to help you stay on the saddle—and they look super sassy with boots. They're at the top of every #HorseGirl's wish list!

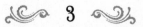 3

And by the way, my real name is Willa, but everyone seems to find that extra syllable just a *liiiiittle* too much effort, so across the universe, I am known as Wills. (Even Amara's *name* soars through the air. Just say it: Amaaaaaara. Now try Wills . . . *thud*.)

But when we're finally at the stable, Clyde doesn't care what my name is or how many times I have gently nudged his flanks, asking him to please, pretty please, *move*. He only cares about staying right here. In this exact spot. For the rest of time.

My tongue flicks out another *click-click*.

Nothing. I lean forward in my saddle, then pull one of his reins to the right, hoping he might turn a little and slide into gear.

"Come on, boy," I whisper as Amara glares at me. "I know you need your me-time, but must it be right now?"

It must, apparently. "I have snacks back at the paddock," I quietly plead. "Carrots! Apples! These all could be yours!"

"Heads *up*!" Amara calls out again—several notes shriller this time—circling around for a second approach.

She's aiming for an oxer jump—two green-and-white-striped rails that can be configured a bunch of ways but are currently staggered so that the front pole is a bit lower than the back—in the center of the ring.

Exactly where Clyde has parked us. Since I've been taking riding lessons for only a couple of months, we aren't supposed to be anywhere near the oxer.

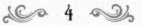 4

Clyde and I are *supposed* to be working on ground poles. That's when my instructor, Georgia, lays a few wooden rails flat on the ground, then Clyde and I practice the steps and pace and positions and *idea* of jumping without, you know, actually jumping.

And we're supposed to get the heck out of the way when the real jumpers come through. That was the first thing Georgia taught us on day one. The *number one, most important, brand-this-in-your-brain* rule. Otherwise, someone could get hurt.

Or worse . . . annoy Amara. Who has just veered around us yet again. (Ugh!!) Even Silver Streak is glaring at me now, nostrils flared.

Then, as if things weren't bad enough, a deep voice rumbles: "Look alive, Wills!"

OMG. It's my dad.

Everyone at Oakwood—Georgia, the other girls taking lessons, the stable hands, several camera-phone-wielding parents, *Amara*, and even (I swear) Silver Streak turn to look at him as he loudly "encourages me" from the side of the ring. OMG. OMG.

"You're blocking traffic, kiddo!"

Oh no, Luis Valdez and Gray Dawson are looking, too! (They're the only boys who take lessons at Oakwood, and they're a grade older than me, but since they don't know I exist, I try to keep the feeling mutual. Plus, if I glance at them, my cheeks liquefy into a shade of extra-hot salsa,

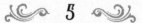

which is *not* a cute look on me.)

I bend toward Clyde's ear, trying to hide my scarlet face in his black mane.

"Clyde, I'm going to tell you a secret," I breathe. "You are the only one in the entire world who can save me right now. *Everyone* is watching us. Are you familiar with the term 'social outcast'?"

There's no response. Guess that's a no. He's too busy enjoying his new career as a frozen ice sculpture.

Amara guides Silver Streak back into position.

"Georgia?" she trills in a sickly sweet voice. "Wills doesn't seem to be paying attention?"

Wait, Amara knows my name? Oh. Of *course* she does, since my dad just blared it across the stable.

"Remember your training, Wills," Georgia chimes in. I take a breath and snap into focus.

"Go!" I command, giving Clyde a firm squeeze with my calves and shifting my weight forward in one last, desperate attempt to save us from certain horse-girl ruin.

By some miracle, Clyde trots forward. Maybe I gave him clearer direction this time, maybe he reconsidered the apple offer, or maybe he's just as afraid of Amara as I am. In any case, we make it out of the way—but just barely. Sweet relief!

Amara and Silver Streak gallop toward the jump—Amara in a two-point position, hovering just above his back. She gathers her reins and leans into his neck, the thoroughbred gracefully lifts his legs in the air, and she sinks closer to him as they float . . . majestically . . . magically . . . effortlessly . . . through the air.

Everyone in the stable stares, spellbound. I hold my breath. The world seems to slow down as I, too, lean forward and shift in my own saddle—soaring vicariously with them.

Except I am now moving. And it is not vicarious.

"Aaaaaahhhhhh!"

Clyde takes off, bounding after Silver Streak.

Apparently energized by a serious case of FOMO, Clyde decides he won't be left behind at the boring ground poles. He strides closer and closer to the oxer as I jostle in my seat, barely clinging to the reins as one of my clumsy feet slips out of its stirrup.

I slide off-kilter, slithering down the saddle leather. Suddenly the arena is zipping past me sideways as Clyde's medium-pizza hooves gallop away. *Galumph-galumph-galumph!*

"*Whoa!*" I yell, tightening my abs and attempting to grip the reins from my diagonal, half-upside-down position.

And just as he's beginning to stretch his neck into a gigantic leap, snatching us both into the Air o' Doom, Clyde—for once—listens to me.

Swooosh!

He slams on the brakes, stopping short and veering left.

My body, still screaming along at full speed, misses the memo, flipping above the saddle and then—*wheeeeeeeee!*—straight over the top rail of the oxer.

And into the dirt. *Thud.*

.

.

.

My first jump!

CHAPTER TWO

Back at my house, I still feel like I'm soaring. My muscles tingle with tiny lightning bolts. (Which could *technically* be the bruise that's forming over my entire body, but I'm going with lightning bolts.) Dad shrugs off his jacket and heads for the kitchen. It's Wednesday night, which means breakfast-for-dinner. *Yessssss.*

"A feast of pancakes," he announces, grabbing a box of Bisquick from the top cupboard and hoisting a spatula in the air. "We flip for horse flips!"

OMG, please don't let that be his new go-to dad joke.

"Hilarious," I say, rolling my eyes and hanging my dusty helmet over my sister's Mathlete sweatshirt in the hall. It's not my fault that Kay has a zillion smarty-pants sweatshirts when we only have four hooks. The math is finally catching up with her.

"You sure know how to make a dismount." Dad grins,

then lifts a wooden spoon triumphantly to join the spatula. "A perfect ten!"

"That's *not* how you score horse jumps," I inform him.[1]

But I'm too zapped from the day's adventures to be truly annoyed. Plus, I never argue when pancakes are at stake.

"I'm just glad you're okay, Wills." His voice drops to an *I'm serious, young lady* tone. "You have to pay attention out there."

"I was!" I groan. "Why aren't you lecturing Clyde Lee?"

"I generally avoid lecturing anyone taller than me—especially when they weigh two thousand pounds."[2] He hacks a slab of butter into the hot skillet, then glances at me, his eyes crinkling. "You should probably clean up before dinner, kiddo. Unless you're going for 'barnyard chic' this evening?"

I catch my reflection in the kitchen window. There are bits of hay scattered in my braids, and large clumps of dirt have infiltrated my braces. It looks like I brushed my teeth with a chocolate bar (#goals). But Dad's right. I could use a good grooming.

---

1   In professional horse jumping, instead of scoring points, you try to *avoid* getting faults—or penalty points. Riders can get faults for taking too long on the course or knocking over an obstacle or having a horse (ahem, *Clyde Lee*) who refuses a jump.

2   Clydesdales can tower up to twenty hands high. (While humans are measured in feet, horses are measured in hands—a fun fact that can be traced back to ancient Egypt.) Twenty hands comes out to about six and a half feet—and that's measuring only to the horse's withers (aka shoulders)! My dad is tall but not *that* tall. I, on the other hand, still have some growing to do . . .

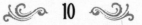

As I trudge up the stairs to my room, a strange feeling rolls over me. I realize I actually, maybe, might be . . . happy? For the first time in a long time.

Sure, Clyde refused the jump. Yes, I somersaulted face-first into the dirt. And yep, after I oh-so-elegantly staggered to my feet, I spit out a mouthful of mud. In front of the entire riding ring.

Amara laughed her perfect, dewy face off. Which meant all the other girls—especially her blond minions, the Claremont triplets—giggled along with her, plus Gray Dawson and some of the snobby parents in the bleachers. I think I even heard some whinnies from the paddocks.

On the upside, Luis Valdez didn't laugh at all; he actually looked a little worried. Or maybe he was just nauseous.

My instructor Georgia made sure I was okay, then told me I had to get right back on Clyde Lee. That's her *number two, most important, brand-this-in-your-brain* rule. So I did. For about two minutes. Then she said I was still looking a little green and maybe we should call it a day . . .

Anyway, the whole thing was completely, 100 percent mortifying. BUT! Georgia says you're not a real Horse Girl until you take your first fall. So, mission accomplished. I am now—mouthful of mud and all—#HorseGirl official!

Unfortunately, I am also #AlgebraTestInTheMorning official.

I flop down on my bed and yank off my size-ginormous boots. *Oooof*, my rump is a little sore from the fall. Actually,

my *everything* is a little sore. I manage to drag my algebra workbook from my backpack, but I can only stare at the cover. I know I should open it . . . but I'm suddenly very, very, *very* sleepy. I lean back into my pillow, just for a moment—

"Don't even think about sitting on anything until you get those clothes in the laundry!" Dad shouts from downstairs.

"I *know*," I grumble, slowly hauling myself upright.

"And I hope you left your boots in the garage!"

"I *did*!" I yell, delicately kicking them under my bed.

I wriggle out of my mud-caked breeches and top, which used to be strawberry pink but now looks like it's been dipped in chocolate. I sniff the shirt to see if I really have to wash it . . . Um, yeah . . . that's gonna need some industrial-strength detergent.

After a good scrub in the shower and a spelunking attempt at flossing my braces, I cocoon myself in a clean, fluffy robe. *Ahhhhh.* I gingerly pick up my stinky riding clothes and toss them down the hallway chute to our laundry room below.

"Heeeeeeyyyyyeeeeeee!"

That ear-piercing shriek is my sister, Kay. She's sixteen, supersmart, and frequently "sensitive" (Dad says that's what we should call it—instead of "cranky" or "emotionally unhinged"). Especially if I come anywhere near her.

"You just threw your disgusting farm clothes on my head!"

"It's not a farm, Kay!"

I slam the chute closed. Then I remember the rest of my point and fling it back open. "It's a *riding academy*."

"Livestock, vile smells, an abundance of manure—what's the difference?" she calls up.

I peek my face down the chute and catch a glimpse of Kay, who's folding a pile of sweatshirts. She has the same dark, frizzy hair as me, and she's also what my grandmother would call "beanstalk tall." But she doesn't try to hide it all the time like I do. She stands (and sits and sleeps and even folds) stick straight—and she wears vintage cat-eye glasses.

"Now my bangs have *horse* on them," she whines. "Wills, you know I'm allergic!"

"Sorry. I thought you were still at quiz bowl practice."

"We finished early," she says, adding a little sneeze for dramatic effect. "And I didn't want to miss breakfast-for-dinner."

The only thing Kay and I agree on is breakfast-for-dinner. She likes geology and geometry and school and homework and trivia and deadlines and show choir and the mythology of Norse gods and irrational numbers and Spanish verbs and snowflake fractals.

I like horses.

My dad says Kay and I should try harder to get along, because we all have to be on the same team right now. It's been a "challenging" year, or at least that's what he keeps calling it. I would call it a "sucky-bad-totally-unfair-awful" year.

My mom is a pilot in the air force, and this summer she got deployed to a base on the other side of the world. It's 7,510 miles from Nebraska, to be precise. Or a fifteen-hour

flight. Or eight time zones, four oceans, and three continents away.

Usually when my mom gets stationed somewhere, we all go with her. So our family migrates a lot, just like geese. Fun fact: Wild horses also move from place to place. Yet geese get all the glory! Sigh.

Anyway, first we lived in Germany when I was a baby, then Texas, then California, and now Nebraska. Nebraska is super different from California—they call freeways interstates here, and there's lots of cornfields, and you have to drive three days to get to an ocean, and everybody waves and says hello to each other, even if they don't really know each other, and other weird things like that.

But this time, my parents decided Kay and my dad and I should stay in Nebraska while my mom's abroad so that Kay can finish high school in the same place she started. They said the matter was *not* up for discussion. Which didn't stop me from discussing it. A lot.

Mom's going to be gone for an *entire* year. And it's only September, so that includes next summer vacation. She won't even be able to come back for long weekends. Or major holidays—like Halloween! Or my birthday. (I asked. Twice.)

I know it's a really big deal that my mom's a pilot—it's a huge accomplishment and an honor, *et ceterahhh*. My parents say that sacrifice is just part of her job. But why can't she have the kind of job where she sacrifices in the same zip code as us?

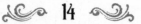

I guess they realized how upset I was, because they finally let me sign up for riding lessons at Oakwood this year. I've gone on a few trail rides before, but these are my first lessons at an official *riding academy*. My parents said it would be a good distraction for me. And it was—because that's where I met Clyde Lee, my favorite distraction in the entire world.

I look up at my herd of Breyer model horses, grazing on the shelf over my bed. Before Clyde, they were all I had to keep me company when we moved to a new city. They may look like "toys" to the untrained eye (or the annoying big sister), but let me assure you—they are *not*.

Breyers are exact, perfect, glorious replicas of the greatest horses in history. And they are kind of a big deal to #HorseGirls around the world.

I've got all the famous racers—like Man o' War and Secretariat—but my favorite is Dream Weaver. He's a beautiful caramel-apple-colored thoroughbred, with long legs stretched out into a full gallop and a golden mane waving in the wind.

During our last move, Dad accidentally set half a piano on top of Dream Weaver's box, and two of his hooves snapped right off. I superglued him back together immediately, but he still kind of has to lean against Secretariat, or he'll topple right over. Which is exactly how sleepy I feel right—

"Dinnnnner!" a familiar voice singsongs.

My breath catches in my chest. Mom! Maybe she's come home to surprise me? Like on one of those internet videos?

"If you don't come down soon, Wills, I'm eating your pancakes."

Oh. It's just Kay.

I taste tears forming in the back of my throat. Kay sounds exactly like Mom, so I get confused when she says something nice. I know Kay misses Mom a lot, too, but does she have to be so "sensitive" all the time because of it? I sniffle, scoop up my homework, and shuffle down the stairs to the kitchen.

Hisssss. The smell of pancakes bubbling in the skillet wafts to my nose and cheers me up, just a tiny bit. My dad glances at me as he flips another hotcake on the stack.

"Have you made any new pals, at Oakwood?"

I bristle, rolling my eyes before he can even finish his sentence.

"First of all, nobody says *pals*," I inform him. "Second of all, I doubt anyone at Oakwood wants to be my pal—I'm the new-girl weirdo who just fell off her horse and almost puked from a mouthful of dirt."

"Very on-brand," Kay smirks. I throw some eye roll her way.

"And third of all, I don't need any pals now that I've got Clyde."

"Got it, got it, and got it," my dad says, turning back to the skillet. "I'm glad you and Clyde are hitting it off. But you still have to work on some human friends, Wills."

I sigh, then plop onto a kitchen chair next to Kay, whose geography textbook is sprawled out into *my* area. But I'm too

wrung out to complain. Except for the sizzle of the pan, it's strangely quiet in the kitchen.

If my mom were here, she'd be singing along with Dolly Parton while Kay and I finished our homework. I miss her singing so much. I miss her calling me Willa, not Wills like everyone else. I miss how she smells—like peonies and fresh nail polish. Mostly I miss having her right here—within hugging distance.

Mom would have told Amara to mind her own business at the stable today. And Kay to stop yelling at me about the laundry falling on her head, because it was clearly an *accident*. And my dad to stop embarrassing me in front of every single person he meets.

"Dig in, ladies!" Dad announces, snapping me out of my daydream. He stuffs his phone in his pocket and slides two piping-hot plates in front of us. Kay smacks her textbook closed as I squeak my chair closer to the kitchen table. She daintily tucks a napkin in her lap, then rolls her eyes as I shovel a giant forkful of pancakes into my mouth.

"Wills, you ready for that math test in the morning?" Dad asks.

Ugh. Can't a girl eat breakfast-for-dinner in peace?

"Arrrmost," I say, adding a crunchy slice of bacon to my mouthful of buttery flapjacks. I shuffle my algebra papers and sloppily pencil in some equations, knocking over the syrup bottle in the process.

(Oops . . . apparently, $x^2 - 22x$ = syrup.)

As I try to wipe up the spill, a piece of ripped notebook paper tumbles out of my book to the floor. I crawl under the table to grab it, but it doesn't look like algebra . . . or my handwriting. I lean in closer. It's a note! Scrawled in sparkly purple ink . . .

Dear W,

You're a better rider than you knew,
Before you fell, you almost flew!
It's you the horses quite adore,
So don't give up before you soar.

—A friend

Whoaaaa. Is this for me? Am I the W in question? I jerk back to my seat and shove the crumpled paper into my book before anyone else notices.

But the note can't be for me—I don't *have* any friends at Oakwood. Except for Clyde, but he hasn't quite mastered penmanship yet. And it couldn't be from Georgia, because she was in the riding ring teaching the whole time I was at the stable . . .

Blergh, I can't think clearly because Kay is droning on about her quiz bowl practice.

"And then Sophia hit the buzzer at the very last second, but she wasn't sure if the answer was the Incas or the Aztecs. So she said the Maya! And the other team tried to say she took too long to get her answer out, but then Mrs.—"

Beep-beep-beep-beep-beep. We all snap our attention to the phone in my dad's shirt pocket, which is now trilling and buzzing with FaceTime chirps.

It's Mom! For real this time!

CHAPTER THREE

Swoosh. My mom's face zaps onto the center of the phone as the rest of us glide up to a small rectangle at the top of the screen. We're all back together—at least in pixel form.

"Helloooo, Nebraska!" she says in her sunny, booming voice. She may be thousands of miles away, but it sounds like she waltzed into the kitchen and landed in the chair next to us. Her dimple-to-dimple smile radiates through the camera, even under the sharp fluorescent light of her bunk.

"*Ooh la la*, breakfast-for-dinner," she coos, ogling the plates of pancakes behind us. "Did you save me a stack?"

My dad proudly flips the screen around so she can see the feast he whipped up. Mom grins and claps her hands in appreciation of his culinary triumph.

As she fills us in on her day, Kay and I lean in closer to soak her up. She's wearing her tan flight suit with all the patches I love—especially the one with the wings above her name.

There still aren't many female pilots in the world—only 10 percent, actually. But my mom says to please call her a pilot. The end. Not a *female* pilot. Just like you wouldn't call someone a *female* rider. (She knows speaking #HorseGirl gets my attention.)

"Mom!" Kay practically bursts. "I get to compete in the Knowledge Maestros quiz bowl next Friday—as a real member of the team, not just an alternate."

"Woo-hoo, Kay! Show those Knowledge Maestros who's boss!"

"Won't your chess club groupies be jealous?" I tease her. Then I realize that Kay actually considers this a compliment.

She smiles broadly—a rare sighting in the wild. Kay and I have the same grin-induced dimples as our mom, and the same dark curlicue hair. My dad's hair used to be dark brown, too, but it's now what he calls, ahem: "Salt-and-pepper—because I like to keep things spicy." It's awkward.

"Mom, Mom!" I interrupt, aware of the minutes ticking away. It's 7:30 p.m. here, which makes it 3:30 a.m. there. Her shift starts at 4:00 a.m., but sometimes she wakes up early to talk with us and, ugh . . . the math is exhausting. The point is, my time is brief and my time is now!

I blurt out the story of my riding lesson and Clyde and the jump and the fall and the mud as quickly as I can.

"Oh, sweetheart, what a day," my mom says, shaking her head. "I'm proud of you for getting back on the horse—literally. Sounds like you're making some friends at the stable?"

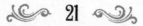

"Did Dad tell you to ask me that?" I narrow my eyes in his direction. But he shrugs in exaggerated innocence.

"I thought these girls at the stable would be your *people*." Mom lifts her eyebrows hopefully on the screen.

"My *people* is Clyde," I reply flatly. "Horse friends are a lot less trouble than human friends."

I consider telling her about the mysterious note in my algebra book, but I stop myself. I don't want to mention it in front of Kay—it would give her enough ammunition to torment me for decades.

It's not the same without you here, Mama, I think. But I don't say that out loud, either, because I don't want to make Mom sad. (Also? I don't want Kay telling everyone at school that I still say "Mama" and have deep talks with my Breyers. Can you imagine if Amara found out? Or Luis Valdez and Gray Dawson??)

Mom bores into me with one of those smiles that's a cross between "reassuring" and "disappointed." Ugh. It's a classic mom trap.

"Willa, I know this move has been tough on you, but you've got to try to make an effort to make *human* friends, too. Too-too-too-too-too-too."

She stutters as the connection fritzes, mid-tooooooo.

"Mom? Are you there?"

But she only grins like a goofy mannequin, motionless on the screen. First Clyde, now Mom. Why is everyone in my life freezing on me today?

"We'll catch you next time," my dad says softly, setting his phone down on the table. We all know my mom's got to get going with her day, just as we're wrapping up ours.

We stack the sticky plates in the dishwasher, then I trudge back upstairs, lugging my homework in my arms. I flick on the lamp by my bed and flop open my algebra workbook. The note is still there, exactly where *someone* stashed it during my lesson earlier today.

I trace the purple letters with my finger. I'm dying to know who this mystery "A friend" is, but I guess I'll have to wait until I'm back at Oakwood to do more sleuthing.

Unless . . . oh no. No, no, no, no, noooo.

"Dad, are you A friend?" I call indignantly down the stairs. My dad bounds up to my doorway, quicker than I expect.

"Of course I'm your friend, kiddo! You can always come to me!" The creases in his forehead deepen. "Everything okay? Is there something you need to tell me?"

Ugh, I've inadvertently triggered his After-School Special Parental Freak-Out Mode. "No, Dad, that's not what . . ." I trail off. "Be honest. Did you leave this in my algebra book?"

I shove the sparkly purple note in front of his face like I'm Nancy Drew catching a bumbling parent red-handed. But he just looks confused. Then guilty.

"Oh shoot, pumpkin. I guess I should have left you some kind of note after your tough day. If your mom were here . . ." Now *he* trails off.

"Dad, come on. It was just a joke. Ha!" I fake a laugh to try to cheer him up.

"I see you inherited my excellent sense of humor," he replies archly, smothering me in a hug. "You know you can always talk to me, right?"

I nod, hoping to end this awkwardness as quickly as possible.

"Okay, then. BTW, don't forget about your homework, kiddo."

"Nobody says BTW out loud."

"*Homework,*" he says. It does not appear to be a joke.

As he heads back downstairs, I exhale in relief. If my dad didn't write the note, this must mean I might, possibly, *maybe* have a real friend at the stable. I fold the paper carefully, then tuck it high on my Breyers shelf, safely under Secretariat's hooves.

I rip out a blank page from my algebra notebook and draw up a list of suspects—it's basically all the students in my Oakwood class, plus Dad and Georgia and Kay.

OAKWOOD FRIEND SUSPECTS

GWYNETH
EVERLEIGH
NOEL
AMARA
GRAY
LUIS
GEORGIA
DAD
KAY

I decide to go through the names one by one. My dad just confirmed it wasn't him, and Georgia was in the riding ring teaching the entire time I was at the stable today, so she wouldn't have had time to get to my cubby and stick a note in my bag. I can safely eliminate both of them.

Next up? Kay. I just realized she was sitting right next to

my algebra book at dinner, where the note was *conveniently* hidden. And this would be just like her, to make me *think* I have a real #HorseGirl friend, then pretend it was all just a figment of my imagination.

I run to the hall and fling open the laundry-chute door. "Kay! Are you pretending to be my ~~friend~~?"

"Why would I pretend to be your friend, you weirdo?" she yells back up. "I'm already stuck being your sister!"

Hmmm. Fair point.

"You promise?" I yell.

"If it makes you stop yelling? Then yes. I promise I am not your friend!"

"Good!" I slam the chute door closed and run back to my room. (Kay may be annoying, but she *never* lies. She says it's unbecoming of a Knowledge Maestro.) I cross her name off my suspect list, along with Dad and Georgia.

Which means: Three suspects down, six to go.

I slide the suspect list under Secretariat's hoof, next to the purple note. I don't have any evidence for any of the other Oakwood riders, so I'll unfortunately have to put this mystery aside until next Wednesday when I'm back at the stable. Because right now I *really* need to focus on algebra. And this time I'm *not* going to let myself get distracted. Or fall . . .

Zzzzzzzzzz.

CHAPTER FOUR

"*Pffffffttttttttt!*" Clyde snorts cheerfully.

"Well, *pffffftttt* to you, too, boy," I reply, brushing his flanks with a currycomb.

He really is happy to see me. That, or he's a little gassy from all the carrots and oat cookies I just fed him. Let the record show that I am not above carb-loaded bribery if it gets Clyde to cooperate when I groom him!

But he deserves a treat—it's finally Wednesday, and I'm finally back at Oakwood. It feels like *forever* since I've been here, even though it's only been, um, seven days.

I rummage through Clyde Lee's grooming bucket for a hoof pick, run my hand down the back of his left leg, and gently pinch the tendon so he'll lift his giant pizza foot.[1]

---

1   Riders are responsible for cleaning out their horses' hooves with a pick. Just make sure your four-legged friend is haltered and crosstied during grooming, in case he's not into the whole pedicure thing.

Still on a sugar high from his carrots, he happily obliges.

"We've got to have a smoother ride today," I warn him as I dig out the dirt, pebbles, and sawdust from the frog of his hooves.[2] "Before last week's lesson, we were basically invisible here."

"*Pffffft,*" Clyde huffs, offended.

"Okay, *I* was basically invisible. Which was fine by me. But now everyone will be staring at us. So, please, no going rogue."

Clyde *pfffffffttt*s again as I squeeze his right hind leg, but he's cagey this time, like he doesn't want me to touch him. It appears he is not 100 percent on board with raising his right hoof—or with my plan.

I lean my body weight into his hip—Georgia says that's how you tell a horse you're serious about the whole "hey, lift your foot up" thing. But Clyde is just as serious about the whole "hey, not gonna lift my foot up" thing.

"Come on, boy—we must mind-meld into one being!" I plead dramatically.

A chorus of snickers echoes behind me. I spin around to see Amara and her three trusty sidekicks—the triplets Gwyneth, Everleigh, and Noel—strolling past Clyde's stall on their way to the arena.

Amara leads the pack, while the other girls trail behind

---

2 Hiding under a horse's hoof is a "frog"—a fleshy V-shaped cushion that acts like a shock absorber. It's important to keep it clean and healthy. (Ribbit-ribbit.)

her like ducklings. She flips her glossy tresses and then aims her dazzling, Cleopatra-esque eyes straight at me.

"Cool shirt?" she says, curling her lips into a tight smile. (It's like Amara is always on *Jeopardy!* Everything she says comes out in the form of a question.)

I glance down at my I RUN ON HORSE POWER tee, mud-splashed breeches, and wild nest of frizz—then gaze up at Amara's impeccably tailored blazer, glittery barrettes, and sleek hair.

"Thanks?" I say nervously. "I made it myself?"

"I can tell!" she says with sugary enthusiasm.

I have a sneaking suspicion Amara is *not* complimenting my crafting skills. (But I can't be sure—she faked me out with an exclamation instead of a question this time.)

"Let's go?" she asks-slash-answers, tossing her hair in the direction of the triplets. "Luis is waiting for me in the riding ring?" As Amara sashays away majestically, Everleigh and Noel quickly follow, giggling in her wake. But Gwyneth pauses for a moment in front of Clyde's stall.

"Don't forget to use the finishing brush on Clyde's forehead . . . most horses adore it."

Amara flips her head around in surprise—clearly astonished that Gwyneth is offering me even the teensy-tiniest bit of helpful grooming advice.

"Gwynnie, are you *coming*?" Amara asks bossily. Gwyneth gives me a half shrug, then hurries to catch up.

I shove my hand back into the grooming bucket. As if any of these girls would actually want to help me. They've all had their very own horses since they were in preschool. Why would they pay any attention to what a common "lesson horse" like Clyde Lee adores? Who says "adore," anyway?

"I *adore* you, Clyde," I mutter into the bucket. The "adore" echoes back and finally hits my brain.

THE NOTE!

Its third line flashes before my eyes:

It's you the horses quite adore.

Whoaaa. Was Gwyneth trying to give me a secret hint just now? Is she A friend? But why would she be nice to me, when Amara—Queen of the #HorseGirls—clearly hates me? Maybe *adore* is just something that everyone at Oakwood says? The same way everyone in Nebraska says "pop" instead of "soda"?

Wow. Only five minutes with Amara and now I can't stop asking questions?

I sweep the stiff dandy brush over Clyde's body in long, steady strokes. It feels good to work out all the grit the currycomb kicked up—and all my frustration at once again being the new-girl-weirdo-outcast with no idea how to make

friends. With the exception of the four-legged kind.

Georgia says any horsewoman worth her spurs knows how to properly groom her steed. She made me practice all the steps before I was even allowed to saddle up. At first I thought it would be tedious, like cleaning my room or staying silent during Kay's endless piano recitals. But it's actually pretty soothing. And it gives me something else to concentrate on for a few minutes, besides my certain social doom.

I carefully comb out Clyde's mane, tail, and the feathers on his feet. I stand just a tad off to the side in case he gets a case of the cranky kicks while I'm combing him. If this were a show day, we'd also shampoo his feathers to get them whipped-cream white, but we can skip that, since it's just a regular lesson. We'll save his professional blowout for when it really counts!

"Lookin' good, mister," I say, raising my phone to snap a quick selfie/horsie of us. Which is what I like to call a #shelfie.[3] Clyde Lee tilts his muzzle ever so slightly and bares his teeth—he knows his angles! Hopefully some other #HorseGirls out there (or at least Mom) will heart it.

After I stash my phone in my pocket, Clyde nudges me again with his muzzle—he clearly doesn't want his spa

---

3   "Shelfie" is a word I invented last week that means a selfie with a horse. Aka a "horsie"—which I also invented. (My sister says I should stop trying to make "shelfie" and "horsie" happen. As if she has any idea what hashtags #HorseGirls like. Stay in your lane, Kay!)

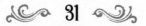

appointment to end. I reach for the soft finishing brush that Gwyneth suggested, running it over his flanks to smooth down his hair. Then I take a deep breath and gingerly pass it over his forehead.

"How's that feel, boy?" I ask anxiously.

He nickers and turns his head back toward me—pushing his snout and lips toward my hair. Ha! He likes it—he's trying to groom me in return! I plant a kiss on his muzzle, which smells like the sweet scent of fresh grass.

"I already took my shower today, Clyde," I laugh. "And I like my frizz just how it is."

Wow. So Clyde really does *adore* the soft brush on his forehead. Maybe Gwyneth really was trying to help me? Maybe she really *is* A friend? There's only one way to find out for sure.

I finish tacking up Clyde, then peek outside his stall to make sure the coast is clear. I tiptoe down the barn aisle, leading Clyde "quietly" behind me. Of course, for each of my hushed tiptoe steps, his ginormous hooves make a ridiculously loud *clomp-clomp*. I glance back and raise my eyebrows at him. Clyde stops—hoof poised in midair. But as soon as I take another silent step forward, his *clomp-clomp*s echo behind me again. Blergh.

We finally reach the stall where Gwyneth's horse, Molasses, lives. I glance inside to make sure it's empty. Phew, it is—they must already be in the riding ring. I crouch down low to get a closer look at Gwyneth's tack trunk.

All I have to do is find something she wrote her name on (I've noticed the girls of Oakwood write their name on *everything*), so I can figure out if the "w" in "Gwyneth" looks the same way as the big purple ⅅ on my note.

Clyde leans his head down low to help me search—but the only "Gwyneth" we find on the outside of the trunk is painted in big block letters with stencils. Double blergh!

I know I shouldn't open the trunk, but I'm desperate to find a label or a notebook or *something* with Gwyneth's handwriting on it. And besides, wasn't she sort of encouraging me to solve the mystery with her "adore" hint earlier?

I whip my head left and right to make sure Clyde and I are still alone in the hallway, hold my breath, then carefully lift the trunk open. *Creeeak.* I paw through bridles, brushes, saddle pads, and crops—poking my head deeper and deeper into the trunk. Clyde leans his nose in, too, sniffing everything carefully as we search desperately for a handwritten "Gwyneth." (I want to sniff everything, too— it smells like . . . expensive.)

Ca-plop, ca-plop, ca-plop.

Clyde and I both freeze, our tail ends sticking out of the trunk. Those exquisitely delicate *ca-plop*s can only belong to the most exquisitely delicate horse at Oakwood: Silver Streak. Which means . . . AMARA IS COMING BACK DOWN THE HALL TOWARD THE STALL!

Red-hot panic and ribbons of sweat wash over me. If Amara catches me snooping in Gwyneth's trunk, my brief career as a #HorseGirl will be over.

I roll into the trunk and pull the lid closed over myself—*clunk*. The sound startles Clyde; he pops his gigantic head in the air and neighs loudly. (For once, his timing is perfect.) After a moment, I prop the trunk lid open ever so slightly with a riding crop, giving myself just a tiny crack of light to see out.

"Clyde Lee?" Amara scolds. "What are you doing nosing around Molasses's stall?"

Despite her condescending tone, she pats his towering neck affectionately.

"Did that silly Wills forget to tie you up?"

I roll my eyes inside the trunk.

"You're looking a little pudgy, boy," Amara continues, rubbing his flanks. "Is Wills feeding you too many carrots?"

Clyde stamps his foot indignantly. Silver Streak, meanwhile, oh-so-delicately paws the hallway floor, eager to get back to the action in the ring.

"Come with us, boy." Amara reaches dangerously close to the trunk lid as she picks up Clyde's reins. "Silver Streak and I will walk you over to Georgia so she can figure out why you've been so . . . neglected?"

Without warning, my nose crinkles and my eyes water. Oh no—I hope I'm not allergic to spying! Or fancy tack. I inhale sharply, a sneeze poised to catapult from my nose.

"Aaah—aaah—aaah . . . ," I wind up softly inside the trunk.

"What's that, boy?" Amara asks, looking curiously into

his saucer-size eyes and scratching his neck behind his ears.

"Pfffffftttttttt!" Clyde snorts happily as I somehow manage to stifle my giant *"chooooo!"* before it comes out.

Clyde then high-steps it toward the riding ring, dragging Amara and Silver Streak with him. I stay frozen in the trunk as the trio *clomp-clomp*s, *ca-plop*s, and *pitter-pat*s down the long hallway.

Finally (several near sneezes later), I hear them all step into the ring. I fling open the trunk, gasping for regular-priced air. After I catch my breath and blow my nose, I notice a small wipe board tacked inside the trunk lid. At the top of the board, handwritten in black marker, are seven giant letters: G-W-Y-N-E-T-H.

Aaaand . . . her name is written in neat slanted print, nothing at all like the ornate swirls and swooping loops on my secret note. Womp-womp.

Great. So I just hurled myself into a trunk, abandoned Clyde Lee, and almost got caught by the Queen of the #HorseGirls herself—all for nothing. Triple blergh!

On the upside? Another suspect down. One mysterious A friend still out there.

CHAPTER FIVE

Thump!

Georgia drops a rail flat on the dirt, just as I hustle into the riding ring on my own two feet.

"Forget something, Wills?" Amara coos haughtily from her seat atop Silver Streak. She points a perfectly manicured finger toward Clyde.

"Sorry, I was, I um, I . . . I . . . ," I stammer, desperate to come up with some plausible excuse for abandoning my horse. "I had a bathroom emergency?"

Thanks a lot, brain.

An explosion of giggles erupts from Gwyneth, Everleigh, and Noel, harmonized by low snickers from Luis Valdez and Gray Dawson.

"Ladies and gentlemen." Georgia shoots a warning look around the ring, and the laughter (thankfully) dies down.

"Next time any of you have an emergency—*of any kind*—

go ahead and ask for some backup," she gently scolds. "You never want to leave a tacked-up horse unsupervised—that's like inviting an octopus into a pottery shop. Either something's gonna get broken or somebody's gonna lose an arm." This is Georgia's *number three, most important, brand-this-in-your-brain* rule.

"Got it," I whisper, staring down at my boots and wishing I could explain that I was actually *spying*, not *bathroom emergency-ing*. Blergh.

When my dad signed me up for lessons, Georgia said I'd be "A-OK" in the Wednesday class, even though the other kids are way more advanced than me. She said it would be better than the Monday class with the kindergartners, but I'm starting to think riding with five-year-olds might be less humiliating.

For now, Georgia simplifies the drills for me as I try (or fail, as the case may be) to catch up. This means that while everybody else gets to jump fences today, Clyde and I are working on cavalletti—or ground poles—again. Emphasis on "ground." No jumping allowed until we nail our footwork (er, hoofwork).[1]

---

[1] Cavalletti are rails that lie either flat or only a few inches above the ground—they're basically miniature fences so that novice riders (like me!) can practice jumping.

"Willa, hop up," Georgia commands, handing me Clyde Lee's reins. Besides my mom, Georgia is the only person on the planet who takes the time to use my real name every now and then.

But I'm so distracted by the trunk diving and the mortifying "bathroom emergency" and everything else that just happened, I forget to concentrate on my mount.

Without thinking, I stick my left boot in a stirrup, then attempt to fling the rest of my body up and over the giant beast. But Clyde's way too tall, even for my daddy-longlegs legs. I only make it halfway, clinging to his flank in a sideways bear hug.

I lose my grip and slip awkwardly down toward his belly—*ahhh!*—just like a baby kangaroo drooping from her mama's pouch.

"Whoa!" Georgia swoops in to catch me. "Wills, you okay?"

"All good!" I say, still hanging upside down.

"You know you gotta use a mounting block or get a leg up with a big boy like Clyde," she reminds me as she helps me to my feet.

"I know," I say. "Sorry."

After I dust myself off, Georgia cradles my boot in her hands and gives me a boost into the saddle. And . . . I'm . . . up. Easy breezy! Except for the fact that the entire class is once again stifling giggles.

Georgia has laid out various groupings of rails flat on the ground for me and Clyde. I mentally measure the distance

between them: three rails squished right next to one another, then four spread out about four human feet (or one giant Clyde step) apart.

"Remember: First walk, then trot, then canter," she instructs. "Don't let him speed up until he's got it. Baby steps."[2]

Right. Sure. Baby steps. What could possibly go wrong?

"You are *not* an airplane," I remind Clyde under my breath. "And we are *not* ready for liftoff."

I gather his reins and gently squeeze his girth to get him moving. He cooperates this time, walking leisurely over each of the poles like it's no big deal—as if last week he didn't swat me off his back like I was a stowaway mosquito.

"Good work," Georgia shouts encouragingly. "Keep your heels down, Willa!"[3]

I straighten up in my saddle, angle my heels lower in the stirrups, and try to anchor my mind in the moment. Clyde remains on his best behavior, pleased with himself, as always.

But when I notice Amara and the triplets circling the

---

2 Horses have four natural gaits, from slow to lickety-split: walk, trot, canter, gallop. For you bongo players out there, walking is four beats, trotting is two beats, cantering is three beats, and galloping is four fast beats. They're the most soothing sounds on the planet!

3 "Heels down!" is something you hear yelled a lot during riding lessons. You're supposed to let your weight fall down into your heels, instead of your toes. It keeps your legs relaxed, your center of gravity low, and your head-shoulders-hips-heels all in a straight line. (Sing it with me: "Heads, shoulders, hips and heels, hips and heels!")

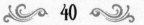

edge of the ring to warm up, my palms (and—yep, there they go—my armpits) begin dripping with sweat.

The triplets' horses all have adorable—not to mention delectable—names. Gwyneth rides Molasses, Everleigh rides Cinnamon, and Noel rides Ginger. I suddenly worry that Clyde might chase after them and try to fly over a jump again, just like he did last week. (I mean their horses *are* named after delicious treats.)

I take a deep breath and remind myself that Clyde is a stable horse—he has done this exercise approximately a million times with a million riders. The majority of whom *probably* didn't get thrown off. At least not two weeks in a row. (Right??)

I wipe my sweaty hands on my breeches and pretend I'm wearing blinders so I can focus completely on Clyde's steps. Instead of on Luis Valdez and Gray Dawson, who are now also warming up on their horses, Valdor and Bentley.

Clyde and I circle the ring, ramping up to a trot over the flat poles. Then we loop around faster, this time in a canter. He hits his strides with confidence, skipping over the rails in rhythm, like we're waltzing. And it *does* feel like we're dancing—his pizza hooves rise high as we swirl across the obstacles, perfectly in sync.

Clyde hops over the last pole with swagger. WOO-HOO! We stayed on course (no jumping detours) and didn't step on a single cavalletti rail.

I bring him to a stop next to Georgia, where he waits for

her appraisal like a dapper gentleman, his nose lifted nobly in the air.

"Well, well," Georgia says. "Clyde finally remembered his manners."

I lean forward to pat his neck, and he swishes his tail as if to say, *You're welcome, ladies*.

"And you got your nerve back, Willa!"

If I had a tail, I would swish it.

"We'll have you jumping real fences in no time," Georgia says, giving Clyde another pat. "I think you're ready!"

CHAPTER SIX

"I think you're ready!"

Amara and I both swivel our heads toward Gwyneth, who's perched atop Molasses. The week flew by in the blink of an eye—it's now once again Wednesday, and we're once again waiting for our turns in the riding ring.

"Um, ready for what?" I ask nervously. What if Gwyneth somehow figured out that I was snooping in her trunk last week and is about to confront me in front of everyone in a dramatic scene worthy of Nancy Drew? I will be forced to melt completely into Clyde's saddle, never to be seen again.

But Gwyneth only grins. "To join the Oakwood Flyers!"

"*Excuse* me?" Amara answers before I can, narrowing her eyes at Gwyneth.

Silver Streak lets out a snort. Even Clyde—who's usually too lazy to bother—perks up his ears.

"Shouldn't you have discussed this with me first,

Gwynnie?" Amara asks-slash-answers. "Since I'm, you know, the team *captain*?"

"Sorry if this is a stupid question," I interrupt, swiveling my head between the triplets and Amara. "But, uh, who are the Oakwood Flyers?"

They all look at me like that was *definitely* a stupid question.

"It's the stable's show-jumping team," Gwyneth explains. "We compete in the Oakwood Invitational each spring, against all the best riding academies in the region."

"It's a really big deal?" Everleigh adds, pulling Cinnamon to a halt next to us.

"We almost always win?" Noel says breathlessly. Her horse, Ginger, stamps emphatically.

The four girls pause expectantly as I raise an eyebrow in confusion. "And you want *me* to be on the team?" My voice cracks as a tiny speck of hope floats up to my throat.

"Well, you're pretty much the only other rider in our class?" Everleigh shrugs.

"Yeah, there aren't really any other options?" Noel explains cheerfully.

"Oh," I say softly, realizing my mistake. "Well, anyway, I'm just a beginner, so I'm probably not ready to compete against one of my Breyers, let alone the, ahem, 'best riding academies in the region.'"

"See?" Amara huffs. "Even *she* admits she's not ready to be a Flyer."

But Gwyneth remains adamant, nudging Molasses

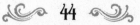

around next to me and Clyde. "Amara, think about it—Wills is learning really quickly. And we need an extra rider for the team to qualify!"

"Gwynnie's right," Everleigh agrees. "We could enter her in the Walk-Trot-Canter equitation class? It's super easy?"[1]

"And the points count the same for the beginner levels as they do for the advanced classes?" Noel adds. "We need good scores from every level if we want to beat the Elkhorn Equestrians?"

Amara now whiplashes her Gaze o' Death around to Everleigh and Noel. They cower in their saddles. Clyde, oblivious to the standoff, swats a fly with his tail.

"So, um, who are these wild Elkhorn Equestrians?" I ask with a laugh, hoping to distract everyone with another stupid question. After thirteen years of living with a "sensitive" Kay, I'm an expert at defusing tension with stupid questions.

"They're basically the richest, snobbiest, meanest team in the entire state?" Gwyneth groans.

"Ha! I would have guessed that was the Oakwoo—"

Gwyneth flashes me a warning look, and I stop myself midsentence.

"The Elkhorn Equestrians stole our best rider last year?" Amara snaps.

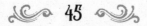 1   Equitation basically means horsemanship. Or horse*woman*ship, as the case may be. In a Walk-Trot-Canter equitation class at a horse show, the *rider* (not the horse) is judged on her form, poise, and performance—while walking and trotting and, yep, cantering. No pressure at all!

"Meghan Marscapone," the triplets sigh in unison.

"They promised Meghan she could be team captain, even though she was *not* ready to be team captain? And she didn't even live in Elkhorn?" Amara is really ramping up now, pacing back and forth on Silver Streak.

"Her parents moved towns so she could switch teams," Everleigh says.

Amara's nostrils flare. "I spent *years* working my way to captain!" (Wow. Amara's so upset that she's not even asking questions anymore.) "Meghan wasn't ready!"

Gwyneth leans in closer to me, as if she's about to reveal a deep, dark secret. "After Meghan took over . . ." She closes her eyes dramatically. "The Elkhorn Equestrians beat us at the invitational."

The Claremont triplets all look down in shame.

"For the first time ever?" Noel whispers.

"Because . . . they . . . *CHEATED*!?" Amara explodes. The horses whinny and swivel their ears—they're as nervous as the rest of us now that we're on red alert for a full Amara meltdown. "It wasn't fair!"

"It was after the Incident." Everleigh nods soothingly, as if this will explain everything.

"The Incident?" I ask.

"It doesn't *matter*?" Amara hisses at me and Everleigh—and anyone else within spitting distance of the northern hemisphere. "I thought I made it clear that we were never going to talk about that EVER again?"

Everleigh's lip begins to tremble. "S-s-sorry, Amara?"

Amara takes a long, cleansing breath, plasters on a smile, and oh-so-politely regrets to inform me: "I'm very sorry, Wills, but as team captain of the Oakwood Flyers, it's my duty to decide who *is* and who *is not* Flyer material."

She stares intently at my handmade tee (IT'S A BEAUTIFUL DAY IN THE NEIGHHHHHBORHOOD). "And you're just . . . *not*?"

I look down at my shirt, suddenly embarrassed by it.

"But Wills flew over the cavalletti poles just now?" Everleigh says timidly.

"Yeah, she's a better rider than we thought?" Noel adds, nervously biting her lip.

"Amara," Gwyneth pleads. "At least give her a chance to try out?"

"Why? So she can fall off her horse again and ruin everything for us?" Amara offers me a dismissive shrug. "I mean, no offense?"

Every cell in my body singes with humiliation. Amara may as well have said: "Wills, you are ginormous and clumsy and weird. Give up all hope now, the end, goodbye!"

Somehow, I force myself to smile back at her. "No offense taken," I answer flatly. "Because I don't want to join the Flyers. Or any other team. Sounds like way too much drama."

Amara's mouth falls open, and she lets out a tiny, insulted "Uh!?"

I *click-click* my tongue at Clyde and trot away toward the other side of the ring.

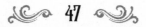

Gwyneth calls after me, but I don't turn around, afraid she might see the tears that have begun to sting the corners of my eyes.

"Gwyneth's right, you know," Georgia drawls, startling me on the other side of the ring. Through my blurry retreat, Clyde and I have wandered over to where she's setting up a fence for the boys to jump. "We could really use a rider like you on the team."

"Georgia, I—"

"Sure, you'd have to start out with the younger riders in the equitation class," she continues, cutting me short. "Showing off all the basic horsemanship you've learned."

"Georgia, I don't want—"

"It's exactly where every student in this class began, just a couple of years ago," she adds with a whistle.

After the lesson, I stick around the stable later than the other kids, grooming Clyde and replaying Amara's cruel words in my mind, furious at her for making me furious. (Who wants to be a stupid Oakwood Flyer, anyway?)

But my brain keeps getting snagged on something else. Everleigh said that I *flew* over the cavalletti—and Noel said I was a *better rider* than they thought. The secret note flashes before my eyes:

Dear W,

You're a better rider than you knew,

Before you fell, you almost flew!

Aha! I knew those words sounded familiar! I may not be joining the Oakwood Flyers, but I'm still dying to know who at the stable left me this note. And more importantly . . . why.

I grab my phone and tap through to a copy of my suspect list.

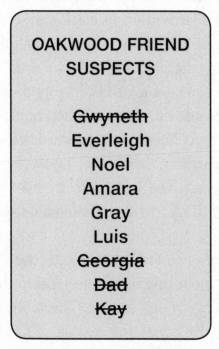

**OAKWOOD FRIEND
SUSPECTS**

~~Gwyneth~~
Everleigh
Noel
Amara
Gray
Luis
~~Georgia~~
~~Dad~~
~~Kay~~

Hmmm. Could Everleigh or Noel be my friend? I was certain they were loyal Amara minions, but maybe one of them took pity on me? Or maybe the note is an elaborate form of reverse psychology designed to trick me? That randomly also happens to rhyme? Blergh, if only I had more evidence . . .

I shove my phone back in my pocket. After saying good night to Clyde, I scurry to the tack room, stow my grooming bucket in a cubby, and hoist Clyde's saddle toward a high hook along the back wall.

Despite my daddy-longlegs legs, I'm still not quite tall enough to reach the hook. I drag a mounting block over and climb on top of it. As I lift the saddle above my head, I notice the name "Clyde" is written in black marker on a label and stuck to the underside of the saddle. Wait a minute.

I suddenly remember that *all* the saddles have name labels. So they don't get mixed up. Georgia wrote out Clyde's saddle label, because he's "just" a lesson horse. But Everleigh and Noel *own* their horses and their saddles—which means they must have written their saddle labels themselves. Which means I can check the handwriting under the saddles of Cinnamon and Ginger to see if it matches the handwriting from the note!

(Have I mentioned I'm a genius detective??)

I shove the mounting block a few feet to the right, under the hook for Cinnamon's saddle. I stretch my gangly arms high and push the handsome seat off the rack, craning my neck to check for a label underneath.

I eventually find it—but the letters are written in neat, slanted black Sharpie. Nothing at all like the elaborate purple curlicues on the note. Blergh!

I delicately plop Cinnamon's saddle back into place, then slide the mounting block over a few more feet, repeating the same inspection of Ginger's saddle. Once again, I find neat, slanted handwriting. Which means Noel is off the suspect list as well. Double blergh!

Which means I've now officially eliminated all the Claremont triplets—triple blergh!

But just as I'm about to put the mounting block away, I catch a glimpse of Silver Streak's pristine saddle—hanging by itself on a side wall. I realize, of course, that there's zero chance that Amara would ever in a million years write me a secret note of encouragement (unless it really *was* reverse psychology??). And yet . . . I won't be able to rest until I can officially cross her name off my list!

Besides, I convince myself, I'm really only going to *look* at Amara's saddle. I'm barely even going to *touch* it! She can't get mad at me for that. (Right??)

I steel myself, then push the mounting block across the room so that it's directly under Silver Streak's hook. I clamber up and gently lift the saddle from its perch. But just as I'm tilting my nose underneath the leather to take a closer look, a voice startles me.

"Wow—for someone who doesn't want to be on my team,

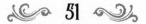

you sure are obsessed with me?"

Amara! *Oh noooooooo!* I twist my body, then wobble on the edge of the mounting block.

"Whoa!" I screech as the heel of my boot slips and I lose my balance, leaning precariously backward. At the very last second, I twist back around and manage to catch myself—by clutching on to Amara's saddle. Which promptly tumbles to the ground. *Thud.*

Amara and I both stare at the now-filthy saddle in semi-horror. Oh no. Oh no. *Oh nooooooooo.*

I look up at her meekly. "I, um, thought you already went home?"

Amara looks at me with undisguised disgust. "So you were just going to *steal* my saddle?"

"No!" I insist, fumbling to lift Silver Streak's precious saddle from the dirt. "It was about to fall from the hook! And I, um, was trying to catch it . . . I think maybe we had an earthquake?"

Blergh, I forgot that I now live in Nebraska, not California. I boost the saddle back up on its hook as quickly as I can.

"See?" I say breathlessly. "Your absolutely unscathed saddle is now officially safe and sound! No harm done. Phew. Okay, then—bye for now!"

And before Amara can say another word, I dash out of the tack room and hustle to the parking lot, where my dad is waiting for me in the car.

CHAPTER SEVEN

"Congrats, kiddo!" my dad gushes as I climb into our car after the lesson, my face still flushed from Amara's angst. Amangst?

After my dad mortified me by shouting "encouragement" from the bleachers, I wasn't taking any chances. I've been making him wait in the car during my lessons. It's basically the dad version of a time-out.

"Congratulations for what?" I grumble, clicking the seat belt over my IT'S A BEAUTIFUL DAY IN THE NEIGHHHHHBORHOOD T-shirt. Ugh. I can't wait to burn it as soon as I get home.

"Georgia just texted me!" Dad answers cheerfully, oblivious to the humiliation I just endured at the stable. "She said you're trying out for the Oakwood Flyers!"

"Um, what? I am absolutely *not* trying out for the Oakwood Flyers."

"Georgia says it will be good for you, help you grow as a

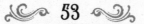

rider." He smiles proudly, then shifts the car into reverse.

"You don't get it, Dad," I explode. "Amara, the captain, doesn't want me on the team. Plus she's super mean. Plus she hates me. Plus she hates my clothes. Plus I'm not good enough."

"Sounds like a lotta pluses there!" my dad says, flipping on the radio. "I didn't hear a single minus!" He is relentlessly, annoyingly optimistic. Ugh.

"Why do I have to try out for a stupid team, anyway? What if I'm more of a lone-cowboy type of horse girl?"

He rolls out of the Oakwood driveway and turns onto the main street. "Wills, I know this year has been rough on you. It's another new city and another new group of kids to meet. But when we signed you up for riding lessons, you agreed you'd at least *try* to make friends. The kind with two legs."

I let out a snort. "You mean the kind who hate me?"

"They won't hate you if they get to know you."

Why is a lame dad compliment somehow worse than the lame dad joke?

"Even if I try out for the team and by some miracle actually make it, I'll just mess everything up at the invitational, and they'll hate me even more than they already do."

"Listen," he says, his tone dropping back to his *I'm serious, young lady* register. "If you want to keep taking lessons at Oakwood, this is *not* up for debate."

"Uh!" I retort oh-so-eloquently. I've been down this road before. Every time we arrive in a new town and I try to make

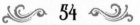

friends, either all the girls make fun of me or we just end up moving. It's usually both. I've realized it's much safer to stick with my Breyers. Or now, with Clyde—who would never, ever, in a million years judge me or laugh at me or accuse me of stealing his saddle.

"I'll make you a deal, Wills," Dad continues, glancing over at me as we stop for a red light. "Try out for the team. If you make it, you have to stick with it through the invitational this spring. Give it an honest shot. If you're still miserable after the big game . . ."

"It's a *show*, Dad, not a game."

"Okay, the big *show*. Then you can quit. But until then, you have to actually make an effort."

"You promise I can quit?"

"You promise you'll make an effort?"

"You promise I can have pancakes every day for dinner next week?"

My dad looks over and frowns. "You can have pancakes *twice* next week."

"You promise—"

"Stop while you're ahead, kiddo," he laughs.

"Fine," I sigh. But a grin breaks through my pout. "I'll try out for the stupid team."

CHAPTER EIGHT

Clomp-clomp, clomp-clomp, clomp-clomp!

Clyde's pizza hooves lumber across the dusty floor of the Oakwood riding ring, slowly but surely gaining momentum. We're heading toward a low fence, which we're actually going to attempt to jump. On purpose this time. I line him up straight for the obstacle.

"Please, please, *please*," I whisper. "I need you to at least *try* to make it over, boy."

I press my gangly legs down into his stirrups and lean forward, hovering slightly above the saddle. And by some miracle, Clyde launches himself into the air at exactly the right moment. We soar—majestically—over the rail, like a slow-motion scene from *Black Beauty*.

(Okay, perhaps "soar" and "majestically" and *"Black Beauty"* are strong words for hopping over a two-foot-tall jump. It may have been more like a scene from a "Hilarious

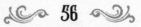

56

Horse Fails" meme. But making it across the fence without either of us eating dirt is *definitely* a miracle.)

"Wooo-hoo!" I exclaim as we clomp down on the other side of the oxer.

I pat Clyde's neck as he slows to a trot and circles to a stop next to Georgia. He lets out a proud *"Pffffffttttttttt,"* shifting his weight to his left side and raising his right hind hoof as if to say *Ta-da!*

"Thatta girl!" Georgia says. "Less mud, more air—I like where this is headed."

I nod and grin, certain my braces are gleaming under the barn lights. I can't believe that only a few weeks ago, Clyde and I were riding on the flat. And a week before that I was eating dirt. Now we're all the way up to . . . knee-high fences!

"Solid jump."

The smooth, movie-star voice rolls in from behind me. I turn my head as Luis Valdez trots by on Valdor. Both of their shiny manes seem to ripple in slow motion. I oh-so-casually lean into Clyde's neck so that Luis won't see my face, which is now the color of marinara sauce.

"Thanks?" I call out from behind the curtain of Clyde's bangs.

Luis looks back at me and nods. "No prob."

Swoon!

"Heads *up*!?" Amara announces, just before she and Silver Streak soar effortlessly (and this indeed qualifies as effortless soaring) over a difficult combination.

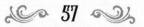

Before I can continue my brilliant, one-syllable banter with Luis and Valdor, Amara and Silver Streak pull up right next to them—as if they're all on a double date. Without warning, Clyde decides to trot after the foursome—he apparently wants to make this a triple date.

"Clyde, *nooooooo!*" I whisper. "We weren't invited!"

But Clyde refuses to be left out of the action. And soon, I'm so close to Amara and Luis that I can't help eavesdropping on their conversation.

"Can't wait to outjump you at the invitational this year?" she teases him, punctuating the sentence with a glossy hair toss.[1]

"Hate to break it to you, Amara," Luis says in his low rumble, "but Valdor has already decided he's going to win the blue ribbon in our jumping class, so there's really nothing I can do about that."

Clyde and I are now trailing only half a horse-length behind them. I tug on his reins, but Clyde appears firmly committed to squeezing in between the other horses' rumps.

"Or maybe Clyde Lee and I will win—hahahaha!"

Oh no. That was *my* awkward, geeky voice chiming in. Amara and Luis turn their heads back, finally noticing that I've been tailgating them. Literally.

---

[1] Unlike most athletic events, men and women compete directly against each other in equestrian events—and so do male and female horses. In fact, it's one of the few sports in the Olympics that's not split up into separate men's and women's divisions—we're all just riders, plain and simple.

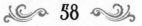

Amara's lips curl into a dangerous smile. "Wills, I thought I made it clear—I mean . . . I thought *you* made it clear—that you're not ready to be an Oakwood Flyer?"

"I changed my mind?" I answer lamely. "Actually . . . my dad said I have to try out for the team if I want to keep taking lessons with Clyde. And I really, *really* like taking lessons with Clyde. Which, of course, who wouldn't? He's pretty awesome." *(OMG, I'm still going. Someone stop me, please!)* "So yeah, I guess what I'm saying is that I *do* want to try out. That is, if you'll let me?"

"Awesome!" Gwyneth says, trotting over on Molasses to join us. "We still have one open spot on the team!"

Amara's eyes land on my T-shirt, and she squints with disdain. It's a sparkly rainbow horse singing into a microphone above the words AMERICAN BRIDLE. "As team captain, it's *my* decision who gets to try out for the open spot?"

"Actually . . . isn't it up to Georgia?" Gwyneth volleys back, her eyebrows lifting.

"Actually—"

"C'mon, Amara, she's doing really good."

Whoa, whoa, *whoaaaa.* Is Luis Valdez actually sticking up for me to the Queen of the #HorseGirls?

"She's doing really *well,*" Amara corrects him. "If that's what you're trying to say, Luis?"

"What I'm *saying*"—*(OMG, he's still going!)*—"is that we could use any points we can get . . . after last year's Incident."

"I know!" Amara snaps, before recovering. She quickly

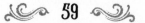

softens her voice. "I just wanted to make sure that Wills is *comfortable* being an Oakwood Flyer—it's an enormous responsibility."

"I'll, uh, do my best?" I ask-slash-answer.

"To be clear, you won't actually be jumping with us at the invitational?" Amara admonishes me. "You'll just be competing in the basic Walk-Trot-Canter class?"

"Um, yeah, you made that pretty clear last Wednesday."

"With the little kids?"

"Yep, I got that part."

"And this is just an emergency situation, you realize?" *(OMG, she's still going.)* "Normally there would be an extremely difficult tryout and—"

"I get it!" I stop her. *(Someone had to.)* "You're only picking me as a last resort."

"Exactly!" Amara actually smiles at me. "And as captain of the Oakwood Flyers, I get to decide what you have to do to try out."

"The deciding part is *my* department," Georgia interrupts, breaking into our #HorseGirl circle. "As the *coach* of the Oakwood Flyers."

Amara first looks startled—then melts into fluttery innocence. "Of course, Georgia! I was just trying to be helpful?" she says. She bats her long lashes.

"Very thoughtful of you, Amara." Georgia nods. "But since you only want Wills to compete in the Walk-Trot-Canter class at the invitational, I suppose we only need to see her walk.

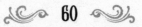

And trot." She pauses. "And maybe canter."

"But, Georgia, don't you think it would be better if Wills had to—"

Georgia ignores Amara, turning back to me and Clyde. "Go on . . . walk, then trot. Then maybe canter."

By now Everleigh, Noel, and even Gray Dawson have all wandered over on their horses, adding to my growing audience. It's now become a full-on "Watch Wills Embarrass Herself during Her Big Oakwood Flyers Tryout" party. Awesome.

Given Clyde's fondness for freezing under pressure, even this super simple challenge makes me nervous. But *(thank the #HorseGods)*, my gentle giant cooperates today, and we complete three laps around the ring: first walking, then trotting, and then . . . cantering.

"Okay, tryout over," Georgia simply declares. "You passed."

I smile gratefully at her. Clyde swishes his tail. Amara, meanwhile, cements her lips into a hard line.

Georgia moseys off to arrange some jumps on the opposite side of the ring, whistling as she works. "Y'all have five minutes to get this team business sorted out before we get started with the lesson," she calls back.

From high on her Silver Streak throne, Amara bestows me with a begrudging nod. "Since you passed your tryout. And because of some *extremely* unfortunate circumstances. And because we have *no* other options." She takes a deep reluctant breath. "I am prepared to offer you a spot on the

Oakwood Flyers. On a *temporary* basis?"

Gwyneth looks over to me expectantly. "Wills, what do you say? Are you in?"

I have a sinking feeling this isn't going to end well. But I promised my dad I'd give it an honest shot.

"Um . . . yeah? I guess so?" (Ugh, only one minute on the team and I'm already answering in the form of a question.)

"Greeeeat." Amara expels the word into a wave of sarcasm.

But Gwyneth seems strangely—*genuinely*—pleased. "Welcome to the team!" she gushes.

"We only have a few months before the invitational," Gray warns me.

"We'll be counting on you," Luis adds in his oh-so-dreamy voice.

Gwyneth looks up, her eyes still dazzling. "I almost forgot! Since you're officially an Oakwood Flyer, you and Clyde can walk in the Halloween parade with us next week! It's our big bonding activity as a team."

Amara's silent Glare o' Death returns.

"Halloween parade?" I ask, nervously biting my lip.

"It's next week, right after our lesson?" Noel explains.

"It's so fun?" Everleigh enthuses. "We dress up the horses?"

"And ourselves?" Noel whispers.

"Oh, yes." Amara smiles smugly. "We all ordered our costumes from the Haute Hoof *months* ago. But I'm sure you'll come up with something *interesting* for Clyde to wear?"

With that, she and Silver Streak swish their manes and walk (mesmerizingly) toward the next jump.

"Just remember, everyone," she adds coolly, looking over her shoulder. "I. Called. Cute."

CHAPTER NINE

"Welp, I'm officially an Oakwood Flyer!" I announce, leaping into the front seat of my dad's car and slamming the door behind me. "I mean, they were one rider short for the team, I was the only one to try out, and Georgia basically forced them to take me. But . . . I'm in!"

"Uh-huh," my dad murmurs into his phone, raising a finger to his lips to shush me. Blergh, he's on a work call. He gives me a dorky thumbs-up to try to make up for his distraction. Supercool, Dad.

"We'll get that to you first thing," he drones on. I click on my seat belt, then fling my riding helmet into the back seat.

"Achoo!"

Oh no. That was definitely the most feared *achoo* on the planet—a Kay *achoo*. I peek back to see that her beloved World History book just took a direct hit from my dusty helmet.

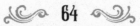

"Sorry," I whisper. "But it only touched your textbook."

"The Byzantine Empire also had dander sensitivity," she hisses, dramatically adjusting her cat-eye glasses and wrapping the book in her arms protectively.

I forgot that Dad had to pick up Kay from her piano lesson today. She has her own driver's license and usually gets to drive Mom's (horsehair-free) car, but it's in the shop. So she's back in the dad-pool with me.

He finally ends his call, slides the phone back into its dorky holster on his belt, and shifts the car into reverse.

"Off we go, with my two favorite ghouls."

"Daaaaaad," Kay and I groan at the same time.

Halloween is still a week away, but he's already dusting off his monster jokes.

"Did you even hear what I said?" I ask impatiently. "I made the Oakwood Flyers team! So you can finally stop bugging me about making human friends."

"I love that you say 'human' like it's a bad word," Kay snorts.

My dad reaches over and tousles my already tangly hair. "That's great, kiddo! They're lucky to have you."

"They're already making me do 'team bonding' activities. Like a Halloween parade next week. Which reminds me, I need a costume for Clyde. But it can't be anything cute."

"Why don't you dress him in one of your T-shirts?" Kay helpfully suggests from behind her textbook. "Those are definitely *not* cute."

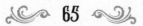

"Kay, this is serious!" I glower at her in the rearview mirror.

"I'm just being honest!"

I turn back to Dad. "All the other girls got their costumes at the Haute Hoof—it's an equestrian shop downtown."

He frowns. "I've never had the pleasure of shopping at the Haute Hoof, but I'm going to guess anything with the word 'haute' is *waaaay* out of our budget. Or anything with the word 'hoof' in it, for that matter."

"But, Dad, that's where everyone else is going!" I plead. "And you were the one who forced me to join the team in the first place."

"Sweetheart, we can barely afford your lessons. Let alone any haute hooves." He sighs and rubs his temple. "You'll just have to come up with a costume for Clyde yourself."

I sigh dramatically. *"Fiiiiine."*

I know Dad's doing his best to juggle everything with Mom so far away. But the Halloween parade is a serious BIG DEAL to the entire stable. And for once(!) I'd like to blend in with everyone at Oakwood, instead of sticking out like a DIY-dork. If Mom were here, she'd understand and come up with a brilliant solution.

But of course, my mom is *not* here. I'm suddenly furious with her. I know that's not fair, but why do I always have to be the one who has to come up with a brilliant solution all by myself? I'm only in seventh grade! I decide that I'm going to text her a *strongly worded* message as soon as we get home.

"When do you need it?" comes a grumble from the back seat.

"What do you mean?" I ask.

"Your little barnyard costume?"

"Just leave me alone, Kay." I cross my arms in front of my chest. "I have enough stress in my life without you mocking me."

"I'll help you make something," she sighs. "I don't want you to break the sewing machine. Again."

I sniffle in disbelief. Do my ears deceive me? Is Kay actually being . . . nice?

"Hey, Kay, that's a great plan!" my dad says, relief washing over his face. "Or should I say, *haaaaaaay*? Like what horses eat. Get it?"

"We get it, Dad." Kay shakes her head. "Please stop while you're ahead."

"But, Kay, you don't even know how to sew," I point out.

"We're not going to *sew* a costume," she says, nudging her glasses higher on her nose. "We're going to *build* it. I'm not treasurer of the Future Engineers of America for nothing."

"Really?"

"Yes, I really am treasurer of the Future—"

"No, I meant . . . never mind. Thank you, Kiki!" I say, reverting to her childhood nickname. I exhale with relief, then feel more tears welling up. Why am I always crying? Even when I'm happy? Blergh.

"OMG, don't make this weird, Wills!" Kay says. But I look

back and see that she's secretly beaming.

"PS." She smirks, dangling a folded piece of paper over my head. "This fell out of your hat."

"It's a *helmet*, not a hat."

"Well, whatever it is, this note fell out of it. And it's addressed to a giant 'W,' so I assume it's for you? But I'm going to have to open it to make sure."

"Noooo!" I squeal, reaching desperately for the note. "That's my private property!"

"What weirdo would be sending a note to you?" Kay grins mercilessly, unfolding a corner of the paper.

"Kay, give it back!" I screech. "Dad, tell Kay to give it back!"

"Kay, hand it over," he sighs, switching lanes. "Or no Mathletes."

Kay groans, then reluctantly tosses the note into the front seat. I quickly snatch it from the floor and jam it deep inside my pocket.

CHAPTER TEN

I dash inside the house, shove my helmet securely over Kay's Spanish Club sweatshirt (OLÉ!) on the coat hook, and sprint upstairs.

"Boots!" my dad hollers.

I sprint back down and kick my boots into the garage, then leap back up the staircase, two steps at a time.

"Your helmet is touching my—"

But I slam my bedroom door before Kay can finish whining. I have a *serious* to-do list to tackle. In no particular order:

1) Catch . . . my . . . breath . . . from all the stairs. I am not a thoroughbred.
2) FaceTime my mom.
3) Come up with Halloween costumes for me and Clyde.
4) Homework: algebra midterm study guide. "A little each night, students." Blergh. Plus I have to work on

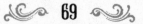

my giant English project, which will take months. Double blergh.

5) Shower? *sniff sniff* Okay, that might need to move up higher on the list.

6) Read secret note!!!!!

I flop on my bed and carefully tug the note from my pocket, now that I'm safely out of Kay's reach. I know I should face my homework first, but . . . that giant ധ is calling my name! (Literally.)

I furiously unfold the neat paper square and see the familiar purple, curlicue handwriting inside . . .

Dear ധ,

Welcome to the flyers team!
Your fellow riders aren't all what they seem.
Keep jumping high, don't lose your head.
And don't let the haters fill you with dread.

—A friend

Interesting. My fellow riders aren't all what they seem. (Is one of them a spy? Or a robot? Or secretly . . . nice?)

"Don't let the haters fill you with dread" sounds like something they'd tell us during our lame middle-school assemblies. But not anything the kids in my riding class would actually say out loud.

"Was it you, buddy?" I ask Secretariat, lifting him from the shelf to keep me company. "Are you A friend?" But he just stares forward, too dignified to respond to my nonsense.

I glance at the clock—Mom! I only have a few minutes to catch her before her shift begins. The only good thing about her being so far away? There's still no "smell" feature on video chat, so I can put off my shower for a bit longer.

I touch her name on my FaceTime contact list, but only get that endless, unanswered chirp. "Mom is not available." (Which, thanks a lot, phone—I am *fully* aware.)

I type out a text to her instead:

> Tried to FT you but you didn't answer 😭 😭

> Guess what??

> I made the Oakwood Flyers! I get to compete in the Invitational. And be in Halloween Parade with Clyde next week!!!

Can you come???

LOL. 😆 😄 I know you CAN'T. Kay is going to help me with my costume?!?!?

😵

I wish you were here. Everything would be sooooo so so so much easier. It's not fair you can't come back. Can you please try???

p.s. Miss you XOXO

I toss my phone on the comforter and return to my latest *A friend* note, tracing the letters with my index finger. Then I remember that I haven't updated my suspect list since I checked the triplets' saddle labels. I reach up to my Breyers shelf and grab it, briskly crossing off Everleigh and Noel.

I consider crossing off Amara's name, too (because—*obviously*), but I didn't get a good look at the handwriting on her saddle label before I fell down. And I'm trying to keep this investigation *professional*.

All I have to figure out is who exactly has access to a purple pen and writes with elaborate curlicues and knows that I exist. That should narrow things down!

"Wills!" Dad yells up the stairway. "Have you finished your homework?"

"Working on it?" I say unconvincingly.

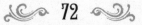

OAKWOOD FRIEND SUSPECTS

~~GWYNETH~~
~~EVERLEIGH~~
~~NOEL~~
AMARA
GRAY
LUIS
~~GEORGIA~~
~~DAD~~
~~KAY~~

"I hope you are, because I'll be checking your study guide right after dinner!"

I guess the rest of my detective work will have to wait until next Wednesday at Oakwood. I stash the note and suspect list back under Secretariat's hoof and crack open my algebra book.

But as I reach for a pencil from my backpack, I catch a whiff of my dirty T-shirt.

Oh boy, that's *baaaad*. Sorry, polynomials, but this qualifies as an odor emergency. As my mom always says: Hygiene before homework.

I robe up and head to the shower, turning the faucet as hot as I can stand it. As the water rushes over me, I think back on the day and, despite everything, can't help smiling.

I, Willa—Peasant of the #HorseGirls—am now officially an Oakwood Flyer! I get to compete in an actual horse show, for actual ribbons, with an actual, real-life horse. Who happens to be Clyde, my favorite person on the planet! And even though Amara still hates me, everybody else on the team seems, well—not to hate me quite as much as Amara?

I could never tell Dad this, but . . . maybe he was right about this whole "joining the team" plan, after all. (Note to self: Definitely do not tell Dad this.)

I emerge from my happy cloud of steam, curl up in my fluffy robe, and shuffle back to my room. Even though I'm exhausted, I flip open my math study guide and review a few equations. As I'm finishing the first page of algebra drills, I hear the unmistakable sound of horses galloping.

It's my ringtone, obviously.

I stay strong and try to ignore my phone—I am, after all, in the polynomial zone. And these equations are not going to solve themselves. Except that the gallops keep coming . . . and my phone is a thundering stampede at this point.

Galumph, galumph, galumph, galumph, galumph!

Wait—what if it's an Oakwood Flyers team message? Or what if A friend is texting me with another clue? Or what if Luis Valdez wants to ask me an important question about my Halloween costume? I mean, he definitely doesn't have my

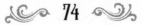

phone number or follow me on social media or even know my last name, but it's *possible* that he was so wowed by my jump today that he tracked me down?

I can't handle the tension—I grab my phone.

But instead of a secret message from Luis, I find a bunch of rapid-fire texts from Mom. Eeeek. I may have been just a *teensy* bit dramatic when I messaged her earlier. Oops?

> I'm sorry I can't be there, Willa. I know it doesn't seem fair now, but I hope you'll understand someday why this sacrifice is so important for all of us.

> In the meantime . . . CONGRATS on making the team!! 💯 🔥 ✨ 🐎 👏

> You and Clyde are going to kick some serious 🐴

> Can't wait to see pics of his costume! 🐎 👻

> p.s. love you both 💚

> p.p.s. did you shower today?? 🔔

I snort out a giggle-sniffle as I read her texts. How many emotions can a girl experience at one time before she short-circuits? I tap out a message back.

> Thanks mom, I 🖤 you. Clyde does too.

Then I force myself to put my phone down and focus on my homework. As I try to solve for x (and W!), my mind wanders back to Amara and why exactly she detests me so much.

Mom says you should try to see the best in everyone, even if everyone isn't showing you their best. She also says that a person can't fly to new heights unless you loan them some wings. Not to be a total nerd (too late!), but maybe I need to find a way to loan some wings to Amara?

Which gives me a genius idea for my Halloween costume . . .

"Breakfast-for-dinner is served!" Dad calls from downstairs.

"Comiiiiiing!" Kay and I shout back in unison.

I run down the stairs, racing to beat her to the table. My costume (and my boring homework) will have to wait until après syrup.

CHAPTER ELEVEN

"Let the Halloween parade begin!" Georgia announces from the center of the riding ring. A sea of parents in the bleachers raise their phones in unison, poised to capture the costumed riders and their steeds.

The air is fragrant with dank leaves and chimney smoke and cozy hay. Fall has to be every #HorseGirl's favorite season. And Halloween at Oakwood has to be the best Halloween in the history of Halloweens.

After our official lesson, we get to dress up ourselves *and* our horses. And take photos of ourselves *and* our horses. And eat special Halloween treats made for ourselves *and* our horses. Triple score!

Amara, of course, leads the parade. She's perched sidesaddle on Silver Streak, beyond glamorous in a high-necked black top, black leggings, and long black gloves all the way to her elbows. The Queen of the #HorseGirls has arrived.

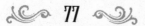

Her neck is draped with piles of pearls (which look suspiciously *real*), while a dazzling tiara gleams from her hair, swept up into a French twist. Silver Streak, meanwhile, is adorned with a silky baby-blue blanket. They walk in a haughty high step—enjoying their moment in front of the parent paparazzi.

"Ladies and gentlemen—Audrey Horseburn from *Breakfast at Tiffany's*!" Georgia says over the PA system, her voice grandstanding with TV announcer reverb. "And Silver Streak is . . . that classic Tiffany Blue Box!"[1]

Amara waves regally to her adoring fans as the parents applaud and cheer (I think there are even some *ooooohs*). I notice my hands are also applauding in the hallway out of habit. Blergh, why would they betray me like this? I quickly tighten my grip on the reins.

"Next up?" Georgia booms. "It's alive, it's alive—it's Frankensteed!"

That's Gwyneth's cue—she trots out on Molasses, whose face and legs have been painted bright green with Pony Paint.[2] Plastic silver "bolts" poke out from either side of his bridle.

"He's ridden, of course, by his beautiful bride."

---

1   *Breakfast at Tiffany's* is a movie from a million years ago (aka 1961) starring actress Audrey Hepburn wearing a little black dress and pearls. It's a favorite costume theme for *cool* girls (aka Amara) and their horses.

2   Pony Paint is a kind of liquid chalk that's totally safe for horses. It washes out with a little shampoo or a good brushing.

Several parents chuckle, pointing to Gwyneth's long white gown and beehive wig—two bright white streaks zigzagging through its jet-black tresses—as it wobbles dangerously above her helmet.

"Uh-oh, we've created a monster!" Georgia singsongs. "And hey, what's brewing over here?"

Everleigh bounces in on Cinnamon—they're wearing matching gauzy black cloaks and pointy witches' hats, a broom tucked lengthwise along Cinnamon's girth.

"I'm spellbound!" Georgia trumpets. "And now I have a serious question: Who's a horse's favorite human? His Mummy Dearest, of course!"

Now Noel darts out on Ginger, both wrapped in white mummy bandages that trail behind them. Once they reach the center of the riding ring, Noel raises her arms straight in front of her, as Ginger halts and lifts one of his front hooves in the air, like they've both fallen into a mummy trance.

"Wow, those two sure are wrapped up in themselves!" Georgia's puns are embarrassing us all, but the parents just keep laughing. "Now, folks, I have a bone to pick with these next two riders . . ."

The boys in our class trot out side by side. Gray has painted intricate white lines on his shiny black quarter horse, Bentley, transforming him into a spooky horse skeleton.

Luis, meanwhile, has buttoned an oversize shirt over the top of his head to make it look like it's been chopped off. (Don't worry, there's a secret mesh panel in the shirt so he can

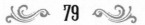

see out—I know because I kept staring at it in the hallway, and then Amara asked me why I was *soooooo* obsessed with Luis, and I had to explain that I *wasn't* so obsessed with Luis, I just wanted to see how his *costume* worked.)

Anyway, Luis is riding Valdor and carrying a fake mannequin head splattered with some gory-looking ketchup. It's pretty awesome, if you're into macabre stuff. Which I totally am.

"Beware, it's the Headless Horseman!" Georgia narrates as the boys circle the ring. "And his accomplice, Mr. Bones!"

"You better *head* them off at the pass!" my dad shouts from the stands, then guffaws at himself.

OMG.

OMGEEEEE!

Why didn't I make Dad stay in the car? He guilt-bombed me with a "this might be the last year I see you dress up for Halloween" speech, which I totally fell for. Mistake! Now he's slinging lame dad puns at Luis Valdez. This is beyond embarrassing.

I wish I had time to banish my dad from the barn, but Clyde Lee and I are up next. We stand by ourselves at the end of the hall, just outside the entrance to the riding ring, waiting for Georgia's cue. Clyde shifts his weight and leans to his left side—he must be as nervous as I am.

I'm wearing my breeches and boots like always, with a plain white button-down and one of Mom's scarves. Her old leather flight jacket hangs over my shoulders, and a pair of

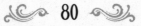

swim goggles stretch across my helmet.

I know it doesn't look like much of a costume yet, but that's only because I kept Clyde's outfit a secret from everyone until the very last moment . . .

Just before we enter the ring, I strap two enormous red cardboard wings onto his flanks. Last night, Kay helped me cut them out from an old TV box in the basement, paint them bright red, and attach them to each end of an old towel. When I drape the towel over Clyde's saddle, the wings balance perfectly on each side.

For the final touch, I clip one of those beanie hats with a plastic propeller into Clyde's mane. *Voilà!*

"And now, coming in for a hot landing," Georgia announces, "the world-famous aviator . . . Amelia Earhart . . . and her trusty airplane, Clyde Lee!"

That's our cue! I nudge Clyde with a squeeze of his flanks. But he only stamps his hoof and gives me a big *"Pfffffftttttttt!"*

This is clearly not his best Halloween in the history of Halloweens.

"Come on, boy," I reassure him. "I know you're shy, but this is going to be fun!"

He remains frozen, shifting his weight in place and uttering another *"Pfffffftttttttt."*

It sounds exactly like a propeller trying—and failing—to start an airplane. He's going to take another crank.

"Let's go, Clyde," I plead. "You've been cleared for takeoff!"

"Ahem," Georgia repeats. "Amelia Earhart and her trusty airplane!"[3]

A few giggles erupt from the bleachers as I miss my grand entrance for the second time. I *click-click* at Clyde more urgently, leaning forward slightly in the saddle.

"*Pfffffftttttttttt!*" he sputters again. This time his engine catches. We have liftoff!

Clyde jaunts into the ring—clearly enjoying his dramatic entrance—as everyone cheers. (I know all the parents are kind of *required* to cheer, but still.) We soar around the arena, Clyde's wings flapping precariously as I post up in the saddle.

"Whoa, did you build that yourself?" Gray asks as I trot past and take my place with the other riders.

"Yep!" I say, flashing my braces in a giant grin.

"So cool!" Gwyneth says.

Luis nods. "Yeah, that's pretty peak."

"So are you—I mean, your *costume*," I stammer. "Not everybody could pull off the whole headless horseman thing."

Amara, sensing the spotlight has mysteriously wavered from her direction, chimes in. "Yeah, that's such a cute idea!?"

---

3   Amelia Earhart was the first woman to fly solo across the Atlantic Ocean—piloting two thousand miles for fifteen whole hours, nonstop. She disappeared in 1937 while trying to circumnavigate (aka "go all the freaking way around") the globe, but she broke all kinds of other records for female aviators before that. AND she inspired my mom to become a pilot. Amelia is a favorite costume theme for *probably-not-cool-but-really-don't-care* girls (aka me!) and their horses.

"Thanks!" I smile up at her eagerly, like a puppy.

Then I remember . . . Amara. Called. Cute.

"But um," I mumble, flailing to save myself, "it's really more *historically accurate* than cute?"

Amara smizes at me. "I was talking about *Luis*'s costume?"

Is that a question? An answer? A warning? A sick burn? The world may never know.

The other kids all seem to be focused on my four-legged airplane. It feels good to be the center of attention for something I built. Instead of, you know, for falling off my horse and eating dirt. Or for being as tall as a Clydesdale. Or for being mortified by Dad.

Who is, as we speak, waving at me enthusiastically from the stands, trying to get my attention.

"Wills, wave your scarf! Like Amelia Earhart did when she landed her plane!"

I freeze in place, hoping he'll give up if he thinks I can't hear him.

"Wills! Photo op! Wave your scarf!" he shouts, more loudly than before.

I consider my options and decide the only way I'm going to stop more mortifying words from tumbling out of my father's mouth is by waving my stupid scarf in the air while he takes a picture.

I sigh, then flick the silk scarf back and forth to appease him. But as I smile for the camera, Clyde whinnies, startled by the whoosh of white flinging past his eyes. He takes a

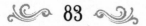

nervous, extra-large-pizza-size step backward, causing one of his enormous cardboard airplane wings to crash into the rump of Noel's horse, Ginger.

Ginger, in turn, lets out a frightened neigh. Her mummy wraps make it hard for her to see—which means she's primed for panic. She rears up into the air, with Noel clinging on for dear life through her own mummy bandages.

The commotion with Ginger startles Everleigh's witch horse, Cinnamon, which startles Luis's "headless" horse, Valdor, which startles Amara's Tiffany Blue Box, Silver Streak—who instantly whinnies and bolts . . .

Right from underneath Amara!

Oh no. And because Amara is elegantly balanced on the side of the saddle, she can't reach her stirrups to dig into and catch herself. Which means that in the blink of an eye, she and her pile of pearls have landed—*plop!*—straight in the dirt.

Oh no, oh no, oh noooooo.

The crowd gasps and rises to their feet. I hurry over to Amara and dismount Clyde, who, of course, is completely unfazed by all the drama we just caused.

"I'm really, really sorry, Amara," I say desperately. "It's just that my dad wanted to take a photo, and Clyde's wings are so big and—"

"Look. What. You. Did!" she hisses at me from the dirt, her tiara tilted precariously out of place. "My costume is *ruined*! I tried to be nice to you—I let you be on the team,

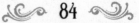

even though you're not ready. I let you be in the Halloween parade, even though you stole 'cute' from me. And how do you repay me for all my generosity? By ruining *everything*—just like I predicted! This was a *giant* mistake!"

I look down at the ground, stunned.

"It was my fault, Amara," Luis's low voice rumbles behind me. "Valdor is the one who spooked Silver Streak. So if you want to kick someone off the team, it should be me."

"Nobody's kicking anybody off the team." Georgia clucks, crouching down to check on Amara.

Amara opens her mouth to say something, then thinks better of it, snapping her lips closed. "Don't worry about it, Luis?" she says, smiling sweetly and adjusting her tiara. "I'm totally fine. And it *definitely* wasn't your fault?"

As she stands up to dust herself off—and glare at me—I notice there's something lying in the dirt, right where all the Oakwood Flyers have gathered.

It's a pen. And it's purple . . .

CHAPTER TWELVE

"My baby!" squeals Amara's mother, clambering over the bleachers and running into the ring, her giant handbag flapping behind. Amara rolls her eyes as her mom throws her arms around her dramatically.

"I can't believe this is happening to you. *Again.* Should we start looking for a different horse? Or a different stable? Someplace with actual *professionals.*"

"I said I'm *fine*?" Amara says, shrugging her off. "Could you try not to embarrass both of us?"

Just as I'm about to ask if anyone happens to be missing a purple pen—Amara's mom spies it, plucks it from the ground, and stuffs it into her mega purse.

"What monster would leave a *pen* in a riding arena? Amara, you could have landed on it and lost an eyebrow!"[1]

 1   Amara's eyebrows are magnificent and she seems to spend a lot of time grooming them, so I have to admit this is a legit concern.

Eeep! That pen was my only evidence! I consider trying to retrieve it. But Amara's mother's handbag appears to be heavily guarded by a cloud of perfume—an airspace I am not brave enough to breach at this moment.

"Enough, Mom!" Amara screeches, stomping toward Silver Streak, whom Georgia has easily corralled and soothed, along with all the other nervous equine mummies and witches and skeletons.

"That will officially conclude our twentieth—and likely final—Halloween parade!" Georgia calls out on the PA, above the hubbub that's now erupting in the ring. "Riders, please join us in the office for refreshments! Parents, please take a deep breath before you email me."

Clyde Lee and I slink out of the arena and back down the hall, as inconspicuously as a giant horse wearing two giant wings and a tiny propeller hat can slink. We're hoping to avoid the wrath of Amara, Amara's mom, and Amara's mom's Purse o' Doom.

But as we reach his stall, I see a strange figure I don't recognize standing in the barn aisle. She's wearing studious metal-framed glasses and a long gray-flecked braid. Clyde hesitates, flicking his ears back and forth. We both sense something's not right.

"Well, this must be the famous Clyde Lee," the woman

purrs, sliding her hand over Clyde's withers and giving him a few pats. He freezes into horse-in-headlights mode.

"And you must be Willa," she says, sizing up my beanstalk-tall frame.

"You can call me Wills," I say stiffly, not trusting her with my real name.

The woman extends her hand to help me dismount. "Sweetheart, you really shouldn't dismount inside a stall—"

"I got it," I interrupt her. (I don't know who this lady is, but I don't want to accept help from someone who looks and talks exactly like the science villain in every comic-book movie I've ever seen.)

I heave my body around to the side of the saddle, then slither down Clyde's flanks, huffing and puffing and eventually dropping the last few feet into a pile of sawdust, which sinks into my boots like quicksand. I wobble back and forth a few times but manage to (barely) stay upright. Ta-da?

It may not be the most dignified dismount in history. I may now have two boots filled with sawdust. But at least I did it all by myself—which is way more than I could say just a few weeks ago.

"You know, it's very dangerous to dismount outside the riding ring," the woman admonishes me. "You could hurt yourself."

"I *know*," I say sharply. "I was, um, having a costume emergency."

I straighten up, adjust my scarf and swim goggles, and

pretend I *meant* to land this way. I always forget exactly how tall Clyde Lee really is. Standing next to him is the only time I feel . . . short? Small? *Normal*. That's the word. Like I belong right in my body and right where I am.

I gaze up at him in gratitude, when a glint of light catches my eye. I turn around. And that's when I finally notice it. There's a stethoscope around the woman's neck.

"I'm Dr. Mansford," she says, gently taking Clyde's lead and stroking his mane. "I came by to watch the Halloween parade—and see what's been bothering good old Clyde here."

CHAPTER THIRTEEN

My heart drops.

"Nothing!" I say protectively, stepping in front of Clyde like a crossing guard. "*Nothing* is bothering Clyde Lee. He's just shy around strangers. And he's ready to get out of his costume. It's *constricting*."

I tug at his cardboard wings, but the towel they're fastened to catches on his saddle. I lean back for leverage, pulling harder on the wings, as if getting them off Clyde *rightthissecond* might somehow stop whatever's about to happen, which I just know is not good.

I hear Georgia whistling behind me—she must have followed me to his stall, which is apparently the hottest spot in the stable post–Halloween parade.

"Lueen," Georgia says, embracing the lady-villain with the braid. "Thank you for coming."

Just then the towel snaps free, sending me stumbling

back and the wings ricocheting—*bonk!*—right on my head.

Clyde lets out a snort. Georgia leans down to check on me. "You okay down there?"

"Georgia, what's wrong with Clyde?" I whisper fervently. "Why didn't you tell me? And who is *she*?"

"*She*," Georgia says, using her regular booming voice and pulling me to my feet, "is Dr. Lueen Mansford, one of the finest horse veterinarians in the entire state. She also happens to be a good friend of mine from a long time ago, when we were both learning to ride."

The vet sticks out her hand. I shake it reluctantly.

"Georgia called me because she's concerned that Clyde here has been showing signs of lameness." Dr. Mansford runs a hand over his withers.[1]

"Lameness?" I narrow my eyes. "Clyde Lee is pretty much the opposite of lame. He is *savage*." Clyde stomps a pizza foot in the dirt as if to emphasize this point.

Georgia chuckles. "Lameness just means a horse has a funky stride or way of standing," she explains. "You notice how when you ask Clyde to walk or change gaits, he's been hesitating? And remember when he refused that jump a few weeks ago? He wasn't just being stubborn. He was letting us

---

[1]   The official definition of lameness in a horse (according to the *Merck Veterinary Manual*): "An abnormal stance or gait caused by either a structural or a functional disorder of the locomotor system. The horse is either unwilling or unable to stand or move normally." The official definition of lameness in a human (according to me): "My dad—any time he's in public."

know something's causing him pain."

"I'm here to sort out exactly what that something might be," Dr. Mansford says briskly.

"Did I ride him the wrong way?" I ask, my eyes widening with fear. "Did I . . . *break* him?"

"Of course not," Georgia reassures me, laughing gently. "I've been keeping an eye on you two, and you're doing just fine. You couldn't hurt a strapping fella like Clyde Lee. This is just a crummy thing that can happen with older horses who've been jumping for a while."

I hesitate. "I did notice that he didn't want to lift his right hind leg when I was trying to pick out his hoof."

"See? That's important to know!" Georgia nods encouragingly. "Being a good horsewoman means being observant. You've got to be your horse's voice."

Dr. Mansford steps toward Clyde's rear legs. "He might have a bone chip, or a bone cyst, or . . ."

She furrows her brow. It does *not* help me feel better.

"Or?" I ask.

"Let's not worry about any more 'or's until Dr. Mansford sorts out what's what," Georgia says, giving Clyde a reassuring pat on his rump.

I stroke Clyde's muzzle and notice my hand is trembling as much as my chin and my lips, which are wobbling as they fight the tears welling up behind my face.

"You're going to be okay, boy," I whisper.

"I didn't want to say anything before the Halloween

parade," Georgia adds, "but Clyde Lee is going to need some time to rest. For the time being, we can't have anyone riding the poor fella."

"How long is 'the time being'?" I ask, panic rising in my throat.

"Maybe a few weeks, maybe a few months, maybe . . ." Dr. Mansford trails off. Then she turns to face me straight on. "Wills, there's a chance that nobody will ever be able to ride Clyde again—it just might not be safe for him."

"Wait—I'm never going to get to ride Clyde again?" The tears I've been holding back break through and pour down my cheeks.

"It's funny, because I didn't hear anybody say that," Georgia says just as my dad walks into the stall. (This is the *worst* Halloween party in the history of Halloween parties, for the record.) "Did you hear anybody say that?" she asks my dad.

"No, ma'am," he says, placing an arm over my shoulder.

"What about you?" she asks Dr. Mansford.

"Not quite." The veterinarian smiles primly.

"Dr. Mansford says there is a *chance*. A chance is not the same thing as a final answer. Do you understand that, Wills?"

I nod, sniffle, then fling my arms as far as they'll go (which is not very far at all) around Clyde Lee's barrel chest.

"You have to keep hope in your heart," Georgia says as I bury my face in Clyde's mane. "We won't know anything until we give Clyde some time to heal. Then Dr. Mansford can run

some more tests. For now, there's no point in wasting your worries."

Before I can protest, Gwyneth pops her head into Clyde's stall.

"Hey, Wills—are you coming to the Halloween party?" she asks impatiently. "We're taking a team photo in our costumes!"

"Great idea!" my dad answers for me. "Go on, kiddo. I'll meet you out in the car when you're done. We need to give Dr. Mansford some more time with Clyde."

I begin to shake my head no, but Gwyneth grabs my hand and drags me out of the stall and down the hall before I can argue. "At least come get a treat for Clyde . . . and yourself!"

CHAPTER FOURTEEN

Crunch.

Inside the front office, I nibble on a horse-shaped cookie covered in sprinkles. The other Oakwood Flyers (except for Amara, whose mother hustled her straight out the door, as if she were a celebrity being hounded by paparazzi) are laughing and gobbling down treats. Fueled by frosting, the other kids seem to have forgotten all about the horse-domino disaster that just happened in the ring.

I, meanwhile, try not to look as glum as I feel. The sprinkle cookie helps—but only a little.

Gwyneth edges closer to me and lowers her voice. "Don't worry about Amara—she'll get over this whole 'falling off her horse' thing. She just freaks out when things don't go absolutely perfectly. And so does her mom."

"It's not just Amara," I sigh, but decide I can't face telling the whole Clyde-is-lame story without risking another deluge

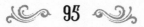

of tears. "Although her mom does seem pretty . . . intense?"

Gwyneth snorts. "That's an understatement! She expects Amara to ride professionally someday. Like as her *job*."

"Oh," I say, chomping down on another cookie. "Is that a thing?"

"Yes, it's a thing!" Gwyneth laughs. "But it's really, really competitive. You have to get recruited by the national team. And after the Incident . . ."

"What's this Incident everyone keeps mentioning?" I interrupt, orange sprinkles now permanently wedged between my braces.

"Shhhh," Gwyneth warns me, glancing around nervously. "If I tell you, you have to promise not to tell *anyone*."

I nod and cross a cookie across my heart.

"So last year, at the invitational—"

But before she can finish, Luis Valdez's fake bloody cranium goes flying between us, bouncing off the cookie tray and rolling under a table.

"Dude, don't lose your head!" Gray snickers, running after the papier-mâché prop from Luis's costume.

As the boys laugh at each other, kicking the head around like it's the funniest thing to happen in history, my mind whirls back to my second ~~friend~~ note.

Keep jumping high, don't lose your head.

OMG. *Don't lose your head.* Could Gray Dawson be my secret friend?

The thought is just plain . . . *awkward.* Gray has barely said three words to me in my entire life. But maybe he prefers to communicate via rhyming secret notes??

Gray lunges under the cookie table, chasing the ketchup-smeared head. I can't stand the suspense any longer. Without thinking, I dive under the table, too.

"Um, Gray?" I ask, just as I realize this was the most awkward plan in the history of plans.

"My name's Mr. Bones," he says, pointing to his skeleton-suit costume before hugging the gory head to his body so Luis can't steal it back.

I cringe. This is *not* how I imagined my big friend unveiling would go.

"Right . . . Mr. Bones. So this is going to sound weird, but . . . do you . . . uh, um . . . could you write down your mailing address?"

His face scrunches. "My mailing address? That's so weird."

"I know. It's just that I, um, want to send you—I mean everyone on the team—a thank-you note! For um, letting me be a Flyer?"

Although he's currently holding a bloody head in his hands, he looks at me like *I'm* the strange one.

"You could just say thanks out loud, dude. It's fine."

"My parents are making me send letters," I fib. "Could you please write it down for me?" Great. If he didn't already think

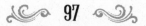

I was a freak show, it is now 100 percent confirmed.

Still, I reach my hand up to the tabletop and grab a paper napkin and a pen from the box Georgia keeps in the office, shoving them toward Gray. Then I sweeten the deal: "I'll address the letter to Mr. Bones!"

"Seriously? Deal!" He grabs the napkin and scratches down a few numbers and letters.

"Thanks!" I say as he crumples the napkin and tosses it back to me.

Then he bolts up, runs toward Luis, and beans him with the fake skull. They both laugh hysterically, like this is the *new* funniest thing to happen in history.

Still under the table, I uncurl the napkin carefully—but the address is written with tiny, harsh capital letters—nothing at all like the glorious script of the last note. Which means . . .

GRAY DAWSON IS NOT A FRIEND.

Phew!

As I sigh with relief, Gwyneth pops down under the table. "Wills?" she asks, tilting her head with confusion. "What are you doing down here?"

"Um, meditating?" I answer lamely. "Anyway, you were about to tell me about the Incident . . ."

Gwyneth shushes me and dives under the table next to me. But just as she opens her mouth to pick up the story again, two pairs of boots stomp over to the cookie table.

"Gwynnie?" Everleigh calls. "Amara needs us at the car!"

"Just give me a sec," Gwyneth calls up from under the table. "I'm, uh . . . meditating."

But Noel leans down and, panicked, tugs Gwyneth out from under the table. "Enlightenment will have to wait . . . Amara needs us *now*!?"

Gwyneth looks back at me and shrugs apologetically as her sisters swoop her away. I stretch up my long arm and snag another horse cookie from the treat table, nibbling away in my secret hiding spot as the party swirls on above me.

CHAPTER FIFTEEN

Later that night, I mope into the house, hooking my helmet haphazardly over Kay's CUT THE CHORDS piano sweatshirt. She looks up from her sea of textbooks on the kitchen table, nudging her cat-eye glasses higher on her nose to inspect my scarf, breeches, and goggles.

"And the underwater lion tamer returns!" she announces sarcastically.

"Kay, you *know* I'm Amelia Earhart," I snap. "You helped me build my costume."

"Slow your propeller," Kay laughs. "I'm just teasing you—try not to be so sensitive."

"Your sister had a tough day," Dad says, dropping his keys on the counter. "Let's give her some *air* while she cools her *jets*."

Ugh. He's officially moved on from bad dad jokes to terrible dad jokes. I don't even bother rolling my eyes at this point.

"So what happened?" Kay asks.

"Hmm, let's see. I made Amara, team captain of the Oakwood Flyers, slip off her horse and fall into the dirt. So she now hates me more than she did before, which I didn't even think was possible. And my only real friend, Clyde Lee, has been diagnosed as lame, so I might never be able to ride him ever again. Mom is still a million miles away. And I got a bloody head thrown at me. Just the usual Wednesday!"

"Wow, that sounds like . . . a lot," she says, flicking her eyes back to her laptop. "I mean, it's not as stressful as cramming for the SATs while simultaneously competing in quiz bowl regionals and memorizing a Chopin piano sonata, but still, pretty stressful for a seventh-grader."

This is Kay's way of being sympathetic—she points out that whatever you're feeling or doing or facing may *seem* rough, but it's nowhere close to as awful as what she, a mighty eleventh-grader, is feeling or doing or facing.

"So who are you going to ride for the big barn show?" she asks.

"It's not a *barn* show, it's a horse show—wait, what do you mean?"

"Well, if your pal Clyde is out sick, who's in?"

While I was busy melting down over Clyde being lame, I'd forgotten that the Oakwood Invitational is only a few months away. Which means I might have to compete in my first horse show without . . . a *horse*. BLERGH!

"I'm sure Georgia will find someone else for you to ride

until Clyde gets sorted out," my dad says, reading my mind. (I hate when his parental telepathy kicks in.)

"But it won't be the same without Clyde," I whine.

"Sometimes, kiddo," he says, wrapping an arm around my shoulder, "life is not the same as it used to be. But that doesn't mean you give up—you recalibrate."

I pull another horse cookie out of my bag and chomp a giant bite from its head. Recalibrating my entire life will require an abundance of snacks.

"Hey, I'm making omelets and pancakes for dinner!" My dad plucks the remaining cookie tail from my hangry clutches. "Save the rest for dessert. And don't forget to unload those cardboard airplane wings from the trunk."

"But I'm still upset about Clyde!" I complain.

"Ah, in that case, I'll just ask our housekeeper to clean out the car," he says, cracking an egg into a bowl before pausing dramatically. "Oh wait—we don't have a housekeeper. Guess it's going to have to be you, kiddo!"

I stomp into the garage and jam the trunk release with my thumb. The tailgate pops open, and I jerk the cardboard wings out from the wayback, letting them flop onto the garage floor.

I spy Clyde's little propeller hat wedged against the back seat. So I climb in, stretching my clumsy fingers as far as they'll reach to snag the bright red plastic blade. But as I reel in my arm, a piece of paper flutters out from under the hat.

It's adorned with a big, fat purple—you guessed it—𝒲. Another note! As I stare at the purple 𝒲, I realize that this note must have been written *before* Amara's mom confiscated the purple pen. I begin to unfold it when—

Galumph, galumph, galumph, galumph, galumph.

It's the muffled, but unmistakable, sound of my ringtone. I reach into my pocket for my phone but come up empty.

Galumph, galumph, galumph, galumph, galumph.

Blergh, it's gotta be here somewhere! Maybe it slipped out of my backpack earlier. I climb over the divider and check the back seat, but I can barely hear the galloping anymore, so I retreat to the wayback, then crawl out in reverse.

Galumph, galumph, galumph, galumph, galumph.

Getting louder . . . I crouch down and tear through the cardboard wings on the floor—where I finally spy a glow from under the left flap.

Galumph, galumph, galumph, galumph, galumph.

Aha! I grab my phone and hit Accept.

Mom!

CHAPTER SIXTEEN

Swooosh! My mom's dimpled cheeks materialize on my phone screen and I instinctively mirror her smile. Sometimes, just seeing her face makes me feel better—even if nothing really *is* better. I launch into a rapid-fire report of my woes.

After listening to my list of worries, Mom tilts her head. "Be patient, Willa. With Clyde, with yourself—even with that Amara person."

"But being patient is impossible when I care about Clyde *sooooo* much!"

"Take a breath, Willa." Her eyes crinkle into a wink. "You just never know how things are going to sort themselves out in the end."

My mom isn't just a "glass half-full" type of person— she's a "glass completely full and there are unlimited refills" type of person. She says that whether you're riding or flying or even just brushing your teeth, you have to be ready for

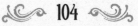

surprises—the happy kind or the sad kind or the refreshingly minty kind. She says if you stop looking for surprises, they'll stop looking for you—and what fun would life be then?

But I'm ready for a break from ALL the surprises. I'm not even asking for a spectacular, glamorous, own-my-own-horse kind of life, like Amara's. I'd be fine with a humdrum, *normal*, borrow-Clyde-for-the-rest-of-my-life kind of life.

A chilly draft rolls into the garage, sending a shiver down my spine.

"Dinner!" my dad calls from inside the house.

"You better get inside and help your dad set the table," Mom says, waving her hand to shoo me through the door. Being late for dinner is *not* an option when you have a mom who's in the military—even when she's on the other side of the world.

I hustle into the kitchen and grab three forks from the drawer, clanging them onto the table and tucking them into tidy paper-napkin triangles. Dad peeks over my shoulder, blowing a kiss to Mom in the phone screen before slinging eggs onto our dinner plates. He grabs a side of pancakes and gently places them on the table next to me. Kay and I devour our omelets while my mom regales us with tales from her bunk.

When she's finished, we all wish her a good night, a good morning, and a good everything in between. And we all silently wish she were here.

CHAPTER SEVENTEEN

The next night—after a rare Thursday breakfast-for-dinner (my dad fulfilled his "pancakes twice in one week" promise)—I attempt to push all the Clyde worries out of my head and be more patient. At least temporarily.

I've been so obsessed with Oakwood for the last week that I've fallen behind with my homework. Or horsework, in the case of my Arabian horse project for English. (We got to pick our own topics, obviously.) The outline is due next week (eek!), and then we have to read our final essays in front of the *entire* class this spring (double eek!), so I need to make it good.

I trot up to my bedroom and begin googling furiously. Fun fact: Arabians are among the oldest and most valiant horse breeds in the world. According to legend, they're so swift that sultans decreed they were created from a desert whirlwind. And they're so beloved that they used to sleep

in their owners' tents so they'd be protected from swirling sandstorms. Or dastardly thieves. And now they compete in endurance races that can stretch up to one hundred miles![1]

I reach up to my Breyers shelf and pull down Rhapsody (an Egyptian Arabian mare) so I can get a closer look at her conformation. I admire her large eyes, delicate muzzle, and high, haughty tail.[2]

I wish *I* could be more like an Arabian—famous for being elegant, strong, and courageous. But let's face it: I am always going to be more like a Clyde—famous for giant-ness and willful and hangry.

If Clyde and I were in an endurance race, we'd pull over to the side of the road, order some ice-cream cones, kick up our feet, and talk about our feelings. Which, to be honest, sounds like a lot more fun than "foraying into enemy camps."

Ugh, I miss Clyde's pizza hooves and his whipped-cream fetlocks already. I even miss the way he cranes his head high into the sky when I'm trying to put his bridle on so I can't reach him—he knows I'll bribe him with a treat to get him to descend to #HorseGirl level. As stubborn as he is, I just

---

[1]   On the day she left, Mom gave me a very old, very beautiful book about Arabian horses. It's called *King of the Wind* by Marguerite Henry. I am now officially obsessed! Did you know Arabian horses' lineage can be traced back almost five thousand years? They're very smart, but also very moody. Reminds me of a certain sister I know . . .

[2]   A horse breed's conformation means how its body is shaped. My grandmother would say *my* conformation is "tall as a beanpole and skinny as a rake." As you can tell, she was extremely helpful to my self-confidence!

can't imagine ever riding anyone else but him.

I tap out a few more sentences of my outline for English, then scroll through my phone as a reward. Looks like Dad sent me that infamous photo he took of me waving my scarf on top of Clyde at the Halloween parade.

Despite the epic disaster that followed this moment he took the pic (i.e., Clyde's giant wings freaking out every horse in the building, causing Amara to get dumped on her rump), Clyde and I *do* look pretty cute in our costumes. I zoom in on Clyde's noble face, with his little propeller hat sitting adorably between his tall rabbit ears, those cursed cardboard wings floating on his sides.

And then something clicks in my memory . . . THE NOTE! How could I have forgotten??

I must have dropped it in the car last night when I was pulling Clyde's wings out of the trunk and Mom called. I was so frazzled by everything that happened at Oakwood that I zonked out immediately after dinner.

Now I zip downstairs, fly through the kitchen (where Kay is still studiously homeworking), and flick the light on in the garage. I dig through the front seat, the back seat, and the wayback, but—there's no note. I search the entire car again, but it's not there. Blergh!

Defeated, I eventually trudge back toward the house. But just before I reach the door, I notice a pile of squished cardboard under the car. Oops? Looks like I forgot to haul the wings down to the basement last night and they got just a teeny-tiny bit *run over*.

I dig through the pile of crumpled cardboard until I find Clyde's mangled propeller hat. And there it is, beneath the plastic hat—the note! I exhale a cloud of steam into the chilly air of the garage and quickly unfold it . . .

Dear W,

I'm watching you on every ride,
You have a special bond with Clyde.
So sad he's hurt, hope he gets well.
Be brave till then, you're doing swell!

—A friend

Wait a second—how does my friend know that Clyde is injured? The purple pen dropped on the ground *before* I found out about Clyde's lameness. Which means whoever wrote this note knew that Clyde was hurt before I did.

Hmm, I scroll through the suspect list in my mind. I've already ruled out Georgia, and the only other person who knew about Clyde being lame was . . . the vet.

Hold up! Is Dr. Mansford my friend?

THAT'S SO WEIRD! She's not even on my suspect list!

But hang on—that literally makes no sense. I only met Dr. Mansford yesterday, so there's no way she could have written the earlier notes. Blergh. Things were *not* this difficult when my only friends were Breyers.

I look back at the note. Hmmm. Something seems different this time. I dash upstairs to my Breyers shelf, where I've kept the other two notes safely hidden under Secretariat's hoof. I lay the three of them next to one another on my bed.

The handwriting on the notes all looks similar, but the slants on the purple W are going in the opposite direction on the most recent note. I lie on my bed and ponder this awhile, then pull Rhapsody and Secretariat down from their shelf to ponder along with me.

There must be *(yaaaaawn)* some sort of *(yaaaaaawn)* clue that I need to . . . *Zzzzzzzzz.*

CHAPTER EIGHTEEN

Crunch. My boots pulverize a pile of crimson, amber, and rust-colored leaves as I walk across the Oakwood parking lot the following Wednesday. I'm wearing my JUST FOR KICKS hoodie—with a unicorn swinging his leg karate style—for courage.

As I swing open the doors of the stable, I steel myself for the post-Halloween wrath of Amara. I take a breath, prepared to face her . . . but instead chicken out and beeline for Clyde's stall.

He whinnies loudly as he spots my frizzy head.

"Clyyyyyde," I coo back, lighting up as I see his beautiful eyes and long giraffe neck. I pet his forehead, then reach into my backpack for the carrots I stashed for him this morning. (My algebra homework ended up a little damp from carpooling with veggies—sorry, polynomials, but we all have to make sacrifices!)

I slide one of the carrots under Clyde's nostrils to see if

he's feeling up for a snack. He gobbles it down like it's the first meal he's had in twenty years. At least we both have our appetites back!

"Take it easy," I laugh, stroking his mane. He pushes his muzzle over my shoulder toward my bag, nickering as he hunts for another carrot.

"Slow down there, big boy," Georgia hollers from the hallway. "You're on stall rest. I don't want you overdoing it. Besides, you're only chowing down on those snacks cuz you're bored."[1]

"Same!" I giggle, popping a piece of leftover Halloween candy into my own mouth.

"So, Ms. Willa." Georgia lifts my carrot-stuffed backpack expertly out of Clyde's reach. "If my math is correct, you're short one horse for today's lesson."

I nod sorrowfully. "I know I can't ride—I just came to the stable because I wanted to check on Clyde."

"Now wait just one minute," she says. "I've got a surprise for you."

My stomach tightens—that same uber-nervous feeling I get when my parents tell me we're going to have to move again. Or on the first day of school . . .

"Meeeeet Minnie!" Georgia announces in her booming emcee voice.

---

1   Vets sometimes prescribe stall rest for horses to make sure they don't move too much or too soon. It's just like being grounded—horses often get bored and resentful and eat their feelings. (Sounds familiar!)

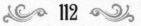

I pop my head out in the stall aisle, look behind Georgia, and see . . . a *pony*?

The sweet creature is barely fourteen hands high—she could practically fit **underneath** Clyde Lee.[2] Her coloring is palomino—a golden caramel color with subtle white dappling, sort of like an undercooked pancake dusted with powdered sugar. She prances toward me, giving a little toss of her mane and a flick of her tail—both of which are buttery blond.

"But she's so, so—" I sputter.

"Glorious? I know."

"Not quite the word I was going for." I glance back at the little pony and let out a little laugh. "I can see why you call her Minnie."

"Yes, ma'am." Georgia grins as she tightens the girth on Minnie's saddle. "The dappling makes it look like she's wearing polka dots. Just like the mouse."

"I meant because she's *tiny*. Literally—her hooves are the size of cupcakes!"

Georgia scrunches her forehead. "You like it when people judge you by your height?"

I shake my head.

"Welp, neither does Minnie." She brushes Minnie's bangs

---

2 Ponies are officially a small breed of horse who are less than fourteen hands and two inches high. A cob is a horse who gets *just* over fourteen hands and two inches but is still really small. Think of them as either tall ponies or short horses. Or just plain adorable.

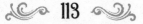

out of her eyes. "And anyhow, she's a Welsh Cob—so she's not *that* tiny. She's smack-dab between a horse and a pony. We rescued her from a family who bought her as a surprise birthday present for a little girl. Turns out that little girl wasn't into mucking stalls or picking hooves. But we got her back on her feet."[3]

"This is all really nice of you, Georgia. But . . ." I lower my voice so as not to offend Minnie. "I consider myself more of a *horse* girl than a *pony* girl."

"Oh c'mon. Minnie's got the giddyup-and-go of a horse twice her size! And this little lady *loves* to jump."

"I'm tall enough to crush her!"

"You want to run through the jumps on your own hands and feet today? Like that woman on the internet?"

I consider *that* possibility and turn back to Minnie.

"It's a pleasure to meet you!" I say enthusiastically, offering the back of my hand for her to sniff.

Clyde brays at the Lilliputian newcomer standing next to his stall, warning her not to get too close to either of us. Minnie brays right back, and Clyde takes a step in reverse, startled by her saltiness. Wow, Minnie's got spunk.

"I feel guilty leaving Clyde alone," I whisper to Georgia.

"You can come see him right after your lesson—you know he'd want you to keep riding, right?"

---

3   Originally bred in Wales, England, Welsh Cobs are fabulous jumpers. They're on the larger end of the pony spectrum, so even though they're small, they believe themselves to be giants.

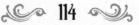

"I guess so," I say, stroking Clyde's withers. "I'll see you soon, boy."

I pat him goodbye, then lead Minnie down the aisle. Clyde stares intently as we walk away, perhaps missing me—perhaps missing my carrots.

"It's good for you to get practice on all kinds of different horses," Georgia reassures me as we stroll down the hall. "If you and Minnie get along okay, you can ride her in the invitational in February."

I turn to look at Minnie and am struck by a pang of guilt. "Can't I ride Clyde at the invitational? Won't he be better by then?"

But Georgia is already whistling her way down the aisle.

CHAPTER NINETEEN

After I lead Minnie into the ring, I give her a "Whoa, girl," asking her to stand still so I can mount up. She cheerfully freezes in place on command. I hoist a foot into her left stirrup and fling myself easily over her saddle. Wow, this is roughly one million times easier than mounting Clyde.[1]

Georgia busies herself in the opposite corner of the arena, setting up fences. I, meanwhile, *click-click* at Minnie, and—wow again!—she immediately starts walking. No nudging, whining, debating, or bribing required. She just . . . *goes*.

As we walk over to join the rest of the team, my gangly legs dangle closer to the ground than I'm used to. Clyde was

---

🐎 1   Traditionally, riders mount from the left side of the horse. A long time ago, soldiers carried swords on their left sides, so they'd mount on the left so as not to drag their sword over their horse's back. These days, a #HorseGirl should learn to mount from either side of a horse, but the left side is still the most popular.

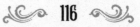

like riding a skyscraper. Now I look like I've climbed onto one of those kiddie rides in front of the grocery store, a grown-up sneaking a turn on the coin-operated pony.

Amara notices us first (because of course she does). A Cheshire cat grin spreads across her face. After a quick beat, she pounces.

"Luis! Gray!" she squeals from atop Silver Streak with undisguised glee. "Have you seen Wills's new *pony*?"

Luis and Gray turn Valdor and Bentley so they're facing me. The Claremont triplets also pivot around on Molasses, Cinnamon, and Ginger.

"Did Clyde get shrunken in the dryer?" Amara asks, throwing her head back to laugh at her own joke.

"Minnie can't help it if she's small," I say softly, quietly defying Amara. (Wow. Maybe Minnie's feistiness is rubbing off on me?)

Amara's lips curl into a hard smile. "Right. Just like you can't help it if you're a giant?"

"You know," comes a deep voice, "I think she's pretty cute. The pony, I mean."

I smile gratefully at Luis, even if it means he has to see my braces. But he quickly trots away on Valdor without glancing back.

"You're so hilarious, Luis?" Amara laughs, hurrying to trot after him.

"Don't worry about her," Gwyneth mutters to me as we circle around the ring—first walking, then trotting, then

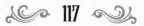

cantering—to warm up. "Amara's just afraid you're going to be a better jumper than she is."

"What?" I laugh. "I'm definitely more of a *faller* than a jumper at this point."

"But you're learning really fast. And she knows she needs you for the team—you're going to do really well at the invitational. Which makes her jealous."

I shake my head. "Amara is, like, the magical fairy princess of riders. She *floats* over jumps."

Gwyneth shoots me a grave look. "You still don't know about the Incident . . ."

"Go ahead and ask Minnie to canter from a halt!" Georgia calls, interrupting us.

"Um, canter from a halt?" I call back. "On Minnie?"

"Yep. That is indeed what I just said. The judges may ask you to do it at the invitational, so you better know your stuff."

Yeah right, I think. Cantering from a halt is a super fancy move to ask from a horse, let alone a pony. Whom I've only met *today*. It involves standing completely still and then sprinting straight into a canter. I've never been able to do it, no matter how many times I've tried with Clyde.

Except . . . this is the new me. The stand-up-to-Amara me. The feisty me! *The Minnie me!* (Ugh, remind me to never repeat that in public.) Perhaps the new me also knows how to canter from a halt?

I tug the reins to slow Minnie down to a stop. Then I touch my inside boot (the one closest to the center of the

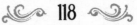

arena) slightly below her girth and give a subtle squeeze.

Woo-hoo—it works! We have canter! Minnie and I whirl around the flat a few times, just to get a feel for each other. She's so much faster than I imagined . . . like a top that's been wound up and finally released. I feel like I'm flying as we zip around the corners of the arena before finally coming to a stop near Georgia.

"Thatta girl!" Georgia says, clapping her hands together. "Looks like we've got a daring duo on our hands."

The triplets look impressed. Amara looks annoyed. Gray and Luis look like they weren't paying attention.

"All right, good warm-up, everyone," Georgia shouts. "Now on to the fences!"

Amara straightens her shoulders atop Silver Streak and sails nimbly over the first crossrail, followed by a vertical.[2] The triplets take their perfect turns next. Then Gray and Bentley take off, stumbling a bit on a roll-top obstacle, but recovering before they completely wipe out.

Finally, Luis and Valdor clear the entire line of jumps smoothly. (Swoon!) I try to give him a thumbs-up, but he zips past me too quickly and I end up thumbs-upping Gray instead. Gray raises his eyebrows and walks Bentley closer to me.

---

2   A vertical jump is one where the poles or rails are stacked straight up and down. They *seem* simple, but they can look like a solid wall to horses, which can intimidate them. (Would *you* want to hurtle yourself as fast as you can toward a big wall?)

"Are you going to have a bathroom emergency again?" His eyes widen, and there's an unmistakable thrill in his voice.

"Gray, I never actually *had* a bathroom—"

Before I can further clarify that I was making a "thumbs-up" sign, not an "I've gotta go" sign, Georgia whistles. "You're up, Wills!"

Wait—wha? I assumed I would be stuck working on the baby jumps again today.

"I want you to give this crossrail a try," she says, indicating a fence that's just a couple of feet above the ground. "It's low enough for you to start on. And Minnie's getting bored on the flat."[3]

"But I've only ridden Minnie for like ten minutes!" I protest.

"Minnie knows what she's doing. And so do you. Best to go now before you overthink it."

I nod. And gulp.

"Remember, whatever you do, don't look down!" (This is Georgia's *number four, most important, brand-this-in-your-brain* rule.) "Keep your eyes on where you want your horse to go next—which is *not* the dirt under the jump."

As if she needed to remind me.

I give Minnie another squeeze. She accelerates into a

---

3   A crossrail is a type of jump where the rails form an X, with the lowest part of the jump smack in the middle. It's rarely used in official competitions, but it's a great beginner jump because it's the easiest for the horse to keep focused on the center of the jump. X marks the spot!

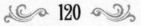

rapid canter as I aim her straight for the crossrail. The fence is low enough to be easy for the more experienced kids—and high enough to induce armpit panic-sweat in me.

But Minnie and I stay focused, sticking with our rhythm as we close in on the jump. She pushes powerfully off the ground in just the nick of time, springing her forequarters into the air . . . as if she just bounced off a trampoline.

I rise into a two-point position and lean forward so that her reins have more give, allowing her neck to stretch up and over the rail. And suddenly . . . we're flying!

I keep my eyes fixed ahead and try to ease down gently in her saddle as we land. Holy smokes! We *landed*!

Like . . . TOGETHER! My second jump!

Wow. I get the feeling I may have underestimated Miss Minnie. And maybe, just *maybe*, myself.

CHAPTER TWENTY

"*Woo-hoo!* Now *that* was a crackerjack jump," Georgia hollers. "Good focus, Wills."

Minnie and I circle around the ring in a jubilant victory lap. I can't stop smiling.

"Georgia?" Amara asks in her dripping-with-honey, just-trying-to-be-helpful voice. "Do you think Wills could be an even *better* jumper if she keeps her heels down?"

I instantly blush beet red but don't give Amara the satisfaction of looking in her direction.

"Ya know, that's something we could *all* work on, Amara," Georgia says sagely, like the #HorseGirl whisperer she is. "Now let's go again. Heels down. *Everybody.*"

I'm itching to ask Georgia if she thinks Amara could be an even better rider if she, you know, *stopped being a horribly mean human being*.

Instead, I concentrate on pointing my heels south and

my toes north and about a zillion other Georgia rules I'm supposed to remember.

I wait my turn as the other riders all attempt the bigger, more elaborate jumps, cutting around corners and swooping back to follow the line of the little course.

Then it's finally my turn again. As elfin as she is, Minnie darts swiftly past the taller horses in the ring, her little legs working double time as we leap over the small crossrail several more times.

If Clyde is my personal frozen statue, Minnie is my personal jet pack. The more we jump, the faster she wants to go—a #HorseGirl could get used to this!

"Sit snooty!" Georgia coaches as Minnie and I trot around the ring. That's her way of reminding me to keep my head up and chest out until we actually get to the jump. All I have to do is pretend I'm Amara with her pin-straight snobby posture—works like a charm!

(I guess there are some benefits to being on a team.)

"Okay, gang, I know this is usually quitting time," Georgia announces as Minnie and I circle the ring. "But before you leave tonight, I think we could all use one more round of jumps. Let's end class on a high note."

Amara and Silver Streak lead the last lap, soaring majestically (sigh) over the line of advanced jumps in perfect rhythm.

"Bravo!" Georgia praises her.

Amara smiles smugly at me, as if to say, *Good luck even dreaming of jumping like that.*

Luis is next, steering Valdor into a steady canter. But as he loops around toward the line of jumps, I also feel myself rotating. Oh no. Oh *noooo*.

Minnie is turning back toward her stall instead of waiting her turn to jump! It's only a few minutes past her usual dinnertime, but she is clearly hungry and ready to eat *rightthisminute*.

"Minnie, stop!" I hiss, pulling back on her reins. "I know we just met. I realize this is your usual suppertime. But we just have to get through one more round of jumps."

Minnie obeys me briefly, then pirouettes again, battling me in a two-step tug-of-war. She is apparently just as afraid of missing a meal as Clyde and I are.

As I struggle with Minnie, Luis and Valdor take off over their final fence. I'm momentarily distracted by them. I let Minnie's reins fall slack as I stare at Luis soaring sublimely over the jump. He makes it look so easy . . . like he's riding a rocking horse . . .

Minnie, obviously embarrassed on my behalf, seizes her opportunity to hightail it for the barn.

"Whoa!" I yell, tugging back on her reins.

Annoyed, Minnie pins her ears back, swats her tail, and rears her legs into a mini kick, trying to buck me off her back so she can get a better spot in the buffet line.

Eeek!

Gravity flings me forward and I face-plant into her flaxen mane. I'm *thisclose* to falling off altogether, but luckily I grab a fistful of her hair and somehow manage to stay on board.

(Georgia's *number five, most important, brand-this-in-your-brain* rule? If you ever feel like a horse is going to throw you, snag a handful of mane and hang on tight!)

"Ooof!" I mumble as I attempt to untangle strands of Minnie's mane from my braces.

"Don't let her get away with that!" Georgia scolds. "Minnie's usually an angel all day, but she gets feisty at suppertime."

(I can relate.)

"I don't think she likes me, Georgia," I sigh.

"I don't really care if she loves you or hates you. If you dismount now, she'll try this little trick every time she gets a little hungry."

I turn Minnie to circle away from the barn, hoping to pull her attention back to me.

"There you go, now ask her to walk," Georgia commands.

I flick out a *click-click*, and Minnie actually listens, walking ahead. Ha! I give her a pat on the neck to encourage her.

"Gooood," Georgia says. "Now get that last jump in before chow time."

I keep Minnie walking forward for a loop around the ring to make sure her brain is focused on the lesson instead of her next meal.

When I'm convinced she's back on track, I give her sides a powerful squeeze to signal I'm ready to trot.

"Pfffffft!" Minnie takes the bit in her teeth and tosses her head in annoyance.[1]

"Easy!" Georgia says. "Willa, that was way too big of an ask for a sophisticated girl like Minnie. She just needs the *tiniest* nudge. Remember, this isn't her first rodeo."

I try again, this time giving Minnie a much subtler squeeze. That's all the spark she needs—she immediately trots forward. I give her another teeny-tiny squeeze to shift her into a canter. *Zoom*—Minnie is ready for blastoff, flying as fast as her adorable cupcake hooves will take her.[2]

"That's the way!" Georgia says. "Do you feel the difference? Now take her over the fence."

Minnie and I line up for the crossrail, and she springs *(boingggg!)* up and over it. She gets so much air that she could have easily cleared the vertical Luis just jumped if we'd been aiming for that instead of the baby crossrail.

"Bam!" Georgia shouts, slapping her thigh.

I grin with pride, my braces glinting under the arena lights.

"And that's a wrap." Georgia whistles. "Now, everybody, including Minnie, can go get some grub."

---

1   A bit is a metal bar that rests across the back of a horse's mouth, in a gap where there are no teeth, and attaches to the bridle. When a horse takes the bit in its teeth, you can tell she's less than happy with her rider and trying to take control of the reins herself. Point taken, Minnie!

2   Once you learn to give your horse clear signals to move or change gaits, you're eventually supposed to make those cues look invisible to anyone watching. The signals should be so subtle that they're imperceptible to everyone but you and the horse. Kind of like your own secret language.

CHAPTER TWENTY-ONE

Slurrrrp. Minnie swipes her tongue along the salt lick hanging on the side of her stall. I untack her as quickly as I can so that she can dig into the buffet of hay and oats the stable hands have laid out for her. Then I hurry down the hall to check on Clyde Lee.

"Pffffffttttttttt!" Clyde paws at his stall to let me know he was *not* pleased about being left behind while I rode Minnie in the ring. All this stall rest isn't helping his terrible case of FOMO.

I kiss his nose and press my forehead against his. "I missed you out there, boy."

He nickers in agreement.

"Minnie was actually pretty fun to ride," I confess. "Like, if you put a saddle on a kangaroo. She's a really good jumper. And superfast. I don't think she even realizes how much smaller she is than the other horses."

Clyde lets out an indignant snort.

"Don't worry, boy," I laugh. "It was *not* love at first sight. She tried to buck me off by the end of the lesson! Minnie just doesn't *get* me the way you do. You're still my fave."

Clyde stares deeply at me with his giant eyes, then nuzzles my frizzy hair until I giggle.

"I thought I'd find you in here," Gwyneth whispers, popping up from behind a stack of hay bales in the stall aisle.

Clyde and I both step back, startled. "Gwynnie, why are you hiding behind a pile of hay?"

Without warning, Everleigh and Noel pop up, too.

"Shhhh!?" they hiss, flattening themselves against the front rail of Clyde's stall like a trio of ninjas, before slipping inside.

Clyde starts to neigh, but Gwyneth quickly slips him an apple. He munches away, happily bribed into silence.

"We were never here, and we're not telling you what we're about to tell you—got it?" Gwyneth steals a glance at the hall to make sure it's empty.

I stare at her for a moment, completely bewildered. But then it hits me—*of course!*

I realize they're finally going to tell me who's been writing me all the secret notes!

"Oh! Got it . . . *Friend*," I answer, winking conspicuously at Gwyneth.

The triplets, however, just stare back at me blankly.

"Wait, what?" Gwyneth asks, tilting her head in confusion.

"Um, nothing?" I answer. (Blergh.)

Before I can further embarrass myself, Gwyneth's face turns serious. "So anyway—if you're going to be an Oakwood Flyer, you need to know about the Incident."

"*Ohhhhh!*" I say. I may not have solved my friend mystery, but this Incident thing sounds pretty juicy. "Go on . . ."

Gwyneth nods, dropping her voice lower. "Last year, just before the invitational, Amara was voted team captain of the Oakwood Flyers. And her mom invited all these US national equestrian team recruiters to come watch her ride."

Everleigh nods. "Amara's mom *really* wants her to become an Olympic show jumper someday."

"And she has *connections*?" Noel adds, flipping her hair for emphasis.

"Wow," I say. "My only connections are to my Breyers."

Everleigh leans in closer. "Oakwood *always* wins the invitational. But last year was the first time we were competing without Meghan Marscapone?"

The triplets fix their gazes on me—apparently waiting for me to grasp the gravity of the situation.

"Meghan was *really* good?" Noel stresses, her eyes widening. "And we lost her to the Elkhorn Equestrians?"

"Oh dear," I say, arranging my face into a worried expression, as if this fact is as deeply troubling to me as it clearly is to the Claremont triplets.

"Last year at the invitational, the Elkhorn Equestrians were basically tied with us," Gwyneth continues.

"Meghan and Amara had both jumped clean in the first round, which meant they had to have a jump-off," Gwyneth explains breathlessly.[1]

"It was so much drama?" Noel adds.

Clyde paws at the stall floor, and Gwyneth tosses him another apple to keep him quiet. "Amara knew she had to have a clean ride *and* finish the course faster than Meghan to keep the trophy at Oakwood. And, of course, impress all those recruiters."

The triplets nod again, like synchronized cuckoo clocks.

"But Amara started getting *really* nervous," Everleigh says. "So her mom gave her this orange electrolyte stuff to drink? It was supposed to keep her focused for the jump-off?"

"It looked *so* nasty?" Noel whispers.

"When it was her turn, Amara jumped the entire course again. She was riding *perfectly*—zero faults!" Gwyneth breathes. "Until the very last jump . . ."

"It was a liverpool?" Everleigh notes.

"Which she's done a million times?" Noel says.

"But then . . ." Gwyneth takes another deep breath, pausing dramatically. "Amara looked over to the stands and saw her mom and the judges and the recruiters and the

---

1   If you "jump clean" in a show, that means you have no faults. You didn't knock over a single pesky rail or go over the time limit. If two or more riders jump clean, they face off in a (dun-dun-dun) jump-off. That means they go through the course again—and the rider with the fastest time (and the fewest rails knocked down) wins.

whole Elkhorn team watching—"

"What's a liverpool?" I interrupt.

Everleigh lets out an exasperated sigh. "It's a fence that has a little pool of water underneath it?" She looks at me as if I should *definitely* know what a liverpool is by now.[2]

Noel sticks a hand on her hip in annoyance. "Can Gwynnie please get on with the story?"

"Of course. Sorry." (Blergh, it feels like I'm always apologizing to somebody for something at this stable. And at my house. And at school. And . . .)

"Anyway!" Gwyneth huffs. "Silver Streak circled around to line up with the liverpool, when Amara's stomach started to rumble a little. At first she thought it was just nerves from all the pressure. So she kept cantering ahead—she knew her time was way faster than Meghan's. All Amara had to do was jump clean over this *last* fence to win the blue ribbon for Oakwood. But as soon as Silver Streak leaped into the air, Amara got this strange look on her face . . ."

Gwyneth closes her eyes and shakes her head. Clyde and I both lean in, willing her to keep going. After another deep breath, she does.

"And then—before any of us could take cover—a giant fountain of electric orange lava erupted out of her mouth!"

"It was super windy so it went everywhere?" Everleigh adds eagerly.

---

2   A liverpool is, indeed, a fence that has a little pool of water underneath it. How cool is that?

"Amara's hair was ruined," Gwyneth says, shaking her head.

"And also her eyebrows?" Noel whispers gravely.

The triplets all wince at the memory.

"It even sprayed over the recruiters!" Everleigh gasps.

"Like if you pumped an orange soda into a lawn sprinkler?" Noel explains.

"I get it!" I say, squishing up my face in disgust. "But *thank you* for the visual."

Gwyneth rubs Clyde's muzzle as he hunts for yet another apple in her bag, then lets out a big sigh. "We lost the invitational for the first time in Oakwood history."

"Wow." I shake my head sympathetically.

But after a moment of respectful silence, I can't help it—I start to giggle. Quietly at first, but the quiet giggles just make me giggle louder. And then louder. And soon, a roar of giggles are shooting out of my mouth.

Have you ever noticed that giggles are more contagious than almost anything on the planet?

Soon the triplets are giggling along with me—it's now a giant tsunami of giggles. We all try to stop, but now it's impossible.

"Come on, guys!" Gwyneth shrieks between fits of laughter. "It's really not that funny!"

"I know! I'm sorry!" I say, doubling over and gasping for breath, because it is actually *achingly* funny. "I'm just imagining Amara spraying those Olympic recruiters . . . with Orange Crush!"

"*Shhhhhhh!*" the triplets keep saying as they convulse with more chortles.

"Now . . . you . . . know . . . ," Gwyneth giggles, trying desperately to catch her breath, "why Amara is so . . . freaked out about . . . the invitational!"

As new waves of laughter roll over us, and fat tears roll down our cheeks, Georgia's voice startles us, booming from down the hall. "I sure hope everyone's finished grooming their horses for the evening."

Blergh! Busted.

The triplets skedaddle back to their stalls. I give Clyde a quick kiss goodbye, then hurry over to groom Minnie. As I pick out her hooves, I try to explain to her why I'm laughing. But I can't stop giggling long enough to get the words out.

Chapter Twenty-Two

"Heads up—center oxer!"

That's *my* voice echoing through the riding ring . . . It's been three months since I officially became an Oakwood Flyer. And Minnie and I have both been giving it everything we've got.

Swoosh. We soar over the jump and land majestically as Amara and all the other kids in our class watch, *mesmerized* by our performance. Or at least that's what I like to imagine.

In reality, Amara is flirting with Luis during my jump, Luis is using his phone as a mirror to check his hair, the triplets are trading hair bows, and Gray is drumming out a song on Bentley's saddle.

But still! Even if nobody was paying attention—I, for one, am proud of myself. Over the last three months, Minnie and I have worked *soooo* hard to get up to speed for the invitational. We've finessed our walking and trotting and cantering for the equitation class. (Which Amara continues to helpfully remind me is the *only* thing I'll be competing in come February 14—*with the little kids*—as she likes to point out.)

Georgia insisted that I keep practicing my jumping this whole time, despite Amara's strong vocal objections. And as of last week, Minnie and I have even tackled an entire course, with a bunch of different fences in a row.

Gwyneth, Everleigh, and Noel have also been helping me, staying late to ride with me and showing me YouTube videos of show jumping so I can watch and learn from the pros. Even Gray and Luis have given me some pointers. (Like "Your horse will relax if you relax." And "Try not to fall!")

To be honest, the holidays were pretty terrible and super hard and super sad here without Mom. Dad made pancakes, and Kay made fudge, and I baked cookies shaped like Clyde. We froze them and sent them all overseas to Mom. But it wasn't the same without her here. So the triplets invited me over to their house a lot to keep my mind off missing Mom. That's when we started our group chat, where we talk about all things #HorseGirls. 🐎 😍

After all this time, I'm actually, *finally*, a teeny-tiny bit starting to feel like a real Oakwood Flyer. And maybe—just maybe?—like I might have found my forever herd.

But wait—I almost forgot the best part of the last three months . . . *Clyde!*

I visit him every single day I'm at the stable, smuggling

him snacks and brushing him with the currycomb. He's getting stronger every day, I can tell. He had to rest in his stall for the first several weeks. But now Georgia has him walking around the ring on a lunge line—and even trotting a little![1]

Sometimes Minnie and I trot right beside him to cheer him on. It's *almost* like riding him. Every night I cross my gangly fingers and toes and make a wish that he'll be better in time for me to ride him at the invitational.

Georgia won't give me a definite yes or a no about riding Clyde yet, but I just know in my heart it's going to be yes! Especially because, *ahem*, I'll only be riding in the equitation class *with the little kids*. What better place for Clyde to make his big comeback?

Even things with Amara are going a *tiiiiny* bit better. Ever since the Claremont triplets explained the Incident and how much pressure her mom puts on her, I actually feel a little sorry for her.

"Pathetic!" Amara's voice ricochets off the barn rafters after my jump.

Welp, so much for me feeling sorry for her.

But Amara seems to be shouting at the entire team, not just at me. She rotates her Gaze o' Shame around the arena,

---

1   A lunge line is a very long rope you can use to exercise your horse without riding him. The horse just circles around you at the end of the lunge while you twirl in the middle. (Lunging is also a good way to check your horse's gait to see if she's showing signs of lameness—or *un*-lameness!)

flips her glossy ponytail, and jams a hand on her hip.

"We are less than two weeks away from the invitational, people! This is our one chance to take back the trophy from those Elkhorn Losers!"

Georgia looks up, clearing her throat pointedly.

"I mean, those Elkhorn *Equestrians*," Amara oh-so-sweetly corrects herself. "But we need to take this show seriously. I'm afraid the rest of you just aren't getting it. I'm seeing sloppy riding, bad rhythm, off-balance jumps . . ."

"All right, Amara," Georgia interrupts. "I'll handle the coaching, and you stick to the captaining. Every person—and horse—on this team has been working their rumps off to get ready for the invitational."

"Of course, Miss Georgia," Amara says, flashing her full-beam smile. "As team captain, I was only trying to offer a little encouragement! You're all going to be brilliant at the invitational! *Right*, guys?"

We all nod nervously.

Later, as we walk back to the stalls, out of Georgia's hearing range, Amara adds icily under her breath: "Do *not* disappoint me."

CHAPTER TWENTY-THREE

Beeeeeeeeep-beep-beep-beep.

After I escape Amara's "inspirational" pep talk, my dad honks for me in the Oakwood parking lot (where I have permanently grounded him). He's been super busy with work lately, so on our way home, he pulls into the McDonald's drive-through and orders breakfast-for-dinner to go.

"Don't forget," I say breathlessly, "the invitational is a week from Saturday. And according to Amara, I better not disappoint her . . . or else!" I flip my frizzy hair and jam a hand on my hip, mimicking the Queen of the #HorseGirls.

"How could I forget, kiddo?" My dad smiles, lifting the greasy Egg McMuffin bag into the car. "Oh, hang on a second. February fourteenth? Is that a Saturday?"

"Yep." I nod.

"Dang it," he says, snapping his fingers. "I've got a work trip to Chicago—I won't get back until late that night."

"But we have to have a grown-up there to sign us in and help carry our tack. Georgia said it was important!"

"I know, sweetheart. I'm sorry—I just, I can't get out of this one. We'll find someone else to take you."

"The invitational is a serious *big deal* in my life, Dad. And you were the one who insisted I join the team! You could at least show up to watch."

Especially since Mom is a million miles away, I say in my mind. Ugh, on the unfair scale, this is SO UNFAIR!

I feel hot tears welling up in my eyes. I glance over at Dad and see his forehead pinched with worry. It actually looks like *he* might cry. And that's even worse than me crying.

"I'm sorry, Dad," I say, trying to crank my voice back into a cheerful register. "I know it's not your fault."

"We'll figure this out, Wills." He passes the steaming fast-food bag to me. "I promise."

(At the sight of the grease-drenched sack, my mouth waters despite myself. No matter how rotten I feel, there are few more heavenly smells than fried hash browns tucked into their little paper envelopes.)

"Kay's upstairs studying," he says as he presses the overhead garage-door button and pulls into the garage.

"Shocking," I say, managing to morph my disappointment into angsty sarcasm. See? Emotional progress!

My dad lets out a deep sigh. "Wills, can you please just ask Kay to come downstairs for dinner?"

I stomp inside, plop the McDonald's bag on the kitchen

counter, and head for the laundry room. I position myself under the chute. "Kay! Dinner!" I shout, my voice echoing upstairs.

The little laundry-chute door above me flips open, and Kay's face appears.

"You! Don't! Have! To! Shout!" she shouts.

"I didn't!" I shout. "We have McDonald's!"

She slams the chute door closed and hurries downstairs. Even the great and mighty Kay is not impervious to the lure of McMuffins. We devour breakfast-for-dinner as Dad apologizes again about not being able to come to the invitational.

"What day's your little pony party?" Kay asks, not bothering to look up from her physics problem set.

"It's not a party, it's a show-jumping competition," I answer curtly.

"What day?"

"February fourteenth, if you must know," I grumble.

"Ah—your perfect Valentine's—filled with livestock and stench!"

"Kay, they're horses, not livestock and besides—"

"I'll take you," she interrupts me, dabbing her napkin to her lips.

I pause, not quite believing my ears. "Is this a prank?"

"You just have to come to my Knowledge Maestros competition first. It starts at nine a.m., but the high school's pretty close to your barn."

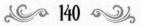

"Oh, Kay, that's a terrific idea!" Dad says, smiling with relief.

"Except we have to have an *adult* guardian," I point out. "And while you frequently act like you're a ninety-year-old grandpa, you're only sixteen."

"I'll write a note giving Kay permission!" Dad claps his hands, thrilled about this new plan.

"But what about your horse allergies?" I ask warily.

"I'll wear a hazmat suit," she deadpans, flipping to another equation on her worksheet. "Just don't embarrass me during quiz bowl."

Okay, so it appears Kay is actually being nice to me. *Again.* Like twice in one year. This must be some kind of record.

I look up at her gratefully. "You won't even know I'm there! Thank you so much, Kay! This really means a lot—"

"Can the 'not embarrassing me' part start right now?" she interrupts. (Which is Kay's way of saying *You're very welcome. I love you.*)

"Oh, I almost forgot," Kay says, lifting her head between nibbles on her fried oval of hash browns. "You got a package."

She points to a small cardboard box on the kitchen counter.

I gulp down the rest of my McMuffin and dash to the box. I haven't gotten a secret note in forever—maybe A friend has upgraded to gifts?!

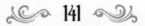

But the package is covered with a plain shipping label from a warehouse, printed in black ink and addressed to *Ms. Willa*. No purple Ⓦ in sight.

I try to peel off the packing tape, first tugging, then digging into the cardboard with my nails, but it refuses to unstick itself. I drop to the floor, wedging the box between my boots for more leverage.

"Get a tool!" Dad calls from the table, shaking his head and handing me a pair of utility scissors from the junk drawer. (This is my dad's *number one, most important, brand-this-in-your-brain* rule: Every job has a tool and every tool has a job. And a *specific* place that tool needs to go back when you're done with said job.)

I slice open the box and bat away the inflatable plastic packing cushions. At the bottom, tucked inside a square of thin tissue paper, I find a stiff cloth patch. It's cut into the shape of wings. Just like the one on my mom's flight suit!

I smile, running my fingers over the embroidered stitches and admiring the golden wings. A typed note flutters out:

Dear Willa,

This patch is reserved for only the most courageous explorers, who fly bravely into new adventures and gallop determinedly into the face of fear. Wear it proudly in your horse show next weekend— and soar over those jumps!

Love, Mama

p.s. Good luck and *don't* break a leg!

I wipe away the tears that are now sneaking under my eyelids. (How do I turn off this emotion faucet?) Even though I'm not technically *jumping* in the show next Saturday, I know the wings will still bring me luck for the equitation competition.

My dad leans over to admire them with me. "Your mom ordered those wings just for you. We'll sew them onto your riding jacket before I leave for my trip."

"But . . . I don't have a jacket, Dad. I was just going to do the show without one."

He crosses his arms and frowns with concern. But I notice the tiniest twinkle in his eyes . . .

CHAPTER TWENTY-FOUR

"You do now!" My dad grins proudly. Like a magician, he unfurls a beautiful tailored show jacket with gleaming brass buttons from behind his back. "Voilà!"

(Even Kay applauds at this dorky dad trick—and her claps only sound *half*-sarcastic.)

"Wait—where did you get this?" I ask, knowing that we could never afford such a fancy jacket.

"Georgia said it's been left in the lost-and-found bin at Oakwood for two years. She declared it 'officially abandoned' and asked me if you might want to adopt it. Looks just about your size . . ."

He holds the show coat up, and I slip my arms inside. My lanky wrists poke out a tad too far from the sleeves, but otherwise it's a perfect fit—my very own riding jacket!

"I love it!" I squeal, flinging my arms around my dad. "Thank you!"

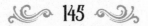

I gallop upstairs to my room to admire the jacket in the full-length mirror. I also admire the hash brown crumbs in my braces, which are going to take some sort of dental-floss trick to lasso out.

As I stare at my reflection, a jolt of excitement runs through me. With the jacket on, I look like a *real* #HorseGirl (at least if you squint). I imagine wearing it while riding Clyde at the invitational. We'll look absolutely *mesmerizing* together!

I raise my phone high in the air to take a pic for my next #HorseGirl #shelfie post. (My freakishly long limbs do come in handy every once in a while!) But as I snap the pic, I feel something scratchy on the nape of my neck.

I slip off the jacket and check the tag. That's when I see it—two letters stitched on the label: "LV."

L . . . V . . .

L . . . V . . . !

(OMG.)

"LV" must stand for . . . LUIS VALDEZ!

O. M. G. Does this mean I am currently wearing Luis Valdez's old jacket? It is officially touching my shoulders. Which used to touch *his* shoulders. Did I mention OMGEEEEEEE?

CHAPTER TWENTY-FIVE

"Bye, Dad!" I shout as I hop out of the car in the Oakwood parking lot. Since it's the middle of arctic February in Nebraska, I'm wearing two layers of long underwear, mittens over my insulated gloves, an extra pair of socks, and my new favorite sweatshirt creation: the silhouette of a horse and a feed bag under the words HAAAAY, GIRL!

"*Haaaay*, girl," Dad says, pouting his lips in exaggerated disappointment. "You're not going to invite me inside to watch your final lesson before the big show?"

"Sorry, Dad—no parents allowed!" I answer cheerily, slamming the car door behind me and dashing into the stable.

(Okay, so maybe that's more *my* rule than Georgia's rule. But I can't have any bad dad jokes distracting me—this is my last practice ride before the invitational. I need to seriously focus!)

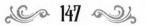

Inside the arena, our lesson goes smoothly. Strangely smoothly. All the Oakwood Flyers seem more intense than usual—but also more energized. Amara yells at us only fourteen times, which is approximately fourteen times fewer than the week before. (#Goals.) The weird thing is? Everyone is strangely . . . *nice* . . . to me. Like, really, really nice. Maybe I really *have* found my herd?

I manage to stay out of the way of the other Flyers as they jump fences, while Minnie and I polish our walking, trotting, and cantering for the equitation competition.

At the end of class, I repeat the same question I ask Georgia every week. "Do you think I can ride Clyde in the invitational?"

Instead of answering "Not sure, we'll have to wait and see," Georgia says, "Maybe." MAYBE! THIS IS HUGE! "But, Willa," she clarifies, "only if Dr. Mansford agrees he's rested and healed enough."

After the lesson, I settle Minnie back in her stall. "Good job out there, girl," I say, scratching her withers. "Now, I hope you won't be too upset, but the thing is, I promised Clyde I'd ride him in my first show—as long as Dr. Mansford says it's okay. I promise I'll ride *you* in the next one. We'll take turns! Like the three horse-keteers!"

Minnie swishes her tail and dives into her dinner, which she is clearly far more worried about than exactly who I'm riding. I hurry over to Clyde's stall to check on him. He bows his head toward me, and I rub the crest of his neck.

"What do you think, boy?" I ask, pointing to my new HAAAAY, GIRL! sweatshirt and twirling around. Clyde admires the shirt with his giant chestnut eyes. And then promptly tries to eat it.

"It's not a snack!" I giggle as he gently nibbles on my sleeve. As I push his head away from my armpit, a shadow falls across the stall door.

"Thought I might find you two in here," Georgia says, leaning against the wooden slats of the stall. She's trailed by Dr. Mansford wearing her dreaded stethoscope.

"Hi there, Willa!" the veterinarian coos at me, as if I'm approximately five years old. "How *are* you?"

I flash her a big smile, excited to finally get some good news. "I'm great!" I say quickly. "Is Clyde all better? Can I ride him for the invitational?"

Dr. Mansford clears her throat. "I did a full examination and took several radiographs—"

My smile falters. "Radio *what*?"

"X-rays," Georgia translates, kicking the dirt with her boot.

"It seems," Dr. Mansford continues briskly, "that Clyde has bone cysts on his right stifle joint,[1] likely exacerbated by his osteochondritis dissecans, or OCD."[2]

---

1   Stifle joints are the joints in a horse's hind limbs. They're basically the horse's knees.

2   Osteochondritis dissecans, or OCD, is a disease that's common to draft horses like Clyde. It affects the cartilage and bones in their joints, and it can trigger bone cysts in their joints. Which are really, really not fun. They can cause pain, resulting in limping and a "reluctance to exercise."

She nods at me expectantly, like this should explain everything.

"I have literally no idea what you just said," I answer anxiously. "Do you mean obsessive-compulsive disorder?"

"This is a *different* kind of OCD, Willa," Dr. Mansford interrupts me. "It's a type of bone disease that can cause pain and damage and swelling."

"Oh," I say softly.

"In an upsetting nutshell," Georgia explains, "our pal Clyde Lee has a bum right stifle."

"Will he be okay?" I ask. I feel my palms turning clammy and my mouth going dry.

"After a few more weeks of taking it easy, he should be absolutely fine in terms of getting around on his own," Dr. Mansford reassures me.

A giant wave of relief washes over me. Followed by a smaller wave of disappointment that I won't be able to ride Clyde at the invitational this weekend. But I try to stay positive.

"That's great news," I say, forcing a weak smile. "I'll just ride him in the next show!"

Georgia rests her hand on my shoulder. "Willa, there's probably not gonna be a next show for Clyde," she says softly. "Unless we do a complicated surgery, he's never gonna be able to jump or be ridden again. Just won't be safe for him."

I start to feel queasy. "So then . . . when can we do the surgery?"

A treacherous silence fills the stall. I look back and forth between Georgia and Dr. Mansford, my eyes pleading for someone to say *something* that makes sense.

"I wish it were that easy, Wills," Georgia says, shaking her head and tracing a circle in the dirt with the tip of her boot.

"It's of course *possible* to try surgery," Dr. Mansford adds. "In the absolutely best-case scenario, there's a chance it would fix everything so that you could ride Clyde as long as you like, even jump him . . ."

My eyes light up at the thought.

But Dr. Mansford looks back at me grimly. "Except that given Clyde's advanced age, there's only a fifty percent chance the surgery would actually work, or that he'd even make it through . . ."

I stare at her in disbelief. "So you're just giving up on him because he's old?"

"Willa." Georgia shoots me a warning glance.

Dr. Mansford takes a deep breath and pushes her braid over her shoulder. "Sweetheart, it might be best if we simply let him retire comfortably now."

At the word "retire," Clyde tosses his head and snorts.

"Clyde is *not* ready to retire. You make it sound like he's a quitter, and he's not!"

"He's a lesson horse, Willa," the veterinarian replies gently. "Not a professional jumper."

Now I'm the one snorting. "He may be *just* a lesson horse to you, but he's *my* everything. Clyde loves to ride and jump.

You can't take that away from him!"

Georgia clears her throat. "Willa, I'm gonna shoot straight with you, because I think you've earned it. This surgery is *very* expensive. Not to mention the rehab, the hospital fees . . ." She lets out a whistle. "At the end of the day, there's only a fifty-fifty shot this thing will work."

Now I stare at Georgia in disbelief.

"The sad truth is," she says, lowering her voice, "Oakwood is barely staying afloat as it is. We've already taken in three rescue horses this year alone. Now, if this were a life-or-death situation, that'd be another story."

"It's *not*," Dr. Mansford says firmly.

"If we spend a fortune on the surgery, then I won't have that emergency money for horses who might be in *real*, life-or-death trouble." Georgia sounds like she's trying to convince herself as much as me.

"But not to worry!" Dr. Mansford brightens (in a way I assume she thinks is comforting but is definitely *not* comforting). "We're already looking for a new home for Clyde where he can rest quietly. Without so many distractions."

My eyes narrow. "You mean he won't even get to stay at Oakwood?"

Georgia looks down. "If we can't use him as a lesson horse, we have no way to pay for his care and food. It might be easier on him somewhere with less hubbub—where he won't feel so left out of all the fun. And Clyde is such a handsome boy, I know somebody will adopt him lickety-split."

I'm so upset, I can't speak, perhaps for only the second time in my life. My head throbs with a sick, stabbing pain. I sputter and blubber over my words.

"But, but—he won't know anyone in a new place. And . . . and nobody will know what snacks he likes!"

"Oh now, he seems to make friends quite easily," Dr. Mansford says cheerfully.

I ignore her and turn back to Georgia. "What about everything you said about keeping hope in my heart? And . . . and . . . about waiting for the final answer and not giving up too soon? Were those all just lies?"

"Of course they weren't lies," Georgia says, shaking her head. "You've always got to keep hope in your heart, Wills. It's just that the exact thing you're hoping for sometimes has to change."

"I am *sick* of everything changing!" I burst into tears and bury my face in Clyde's mane. He drapes his head over me protectively so that I'm tucked under his neck.

"Um, is everything okay in here, Georgia?" a perky voice trills from the aisle. "Did you tell her yet?"

From the corner of my eye, through the curtain of Clyde's mane, I see Amara's glossy ponytail bobbing outside the stall. She's trailed by her triplet groupies.

And that's when I realize—*of course*—why all the Flyers

were so ridiculously nice to me during the lesson today. They already knew about Clyde.

"Go *away*," I whimper.

"Wills, are you okay?" Gwyneth asks softly.

"We're all worried?" Everleigh adds.

"*Really* worried?" Noel whispers.

"There was so much crying we were afraid you might have fallen off your horse again!?" Amara says, with overdramatic concern.

I whip Clyde's mane out of my eyes. "You don't have to worry about me falling ever again, Amara," I say coldly. "Because as of today, I quit the team. If Clyde can't stay at Oakwood, I don't want to stay here, either."

"Wills, you don't mean that," Gwyneth says, startled. "The invitational is only three days away."

"I *do* mean it," I say, my jaw tightening.

Georgia shoos Amara and the triplets away from the stall. "Maybe come back a little later, girls. Willa is dealing with some very tough news right now."

She crouches next to me. "The thing about loving horses, Willa, is that they will eventually—every last one of 'em—break your heart," she says quietly. "But if you're a real horsewoman, you get brave enough to go ahead and love 'em anyway."

I stay frozen, clinging tightly to Clyde Lee. Georgia pats my shoulder before she and Dr. Mansford step out of the stall.

"Take as long as you need and have a good cry," Georgia says. "I know this is a real rough break, Wills. But I promise—

we won't start looking for a new home for Clyde until *after* the invitational."

Clyde heaves a heavy sigh, still draped over my shoulder. I wait until Georgia and Dr. Mansford are out of earshot before whispering in his ear.

"Don't worry, Clyde. I'm not going to let anyone take you away from your home. I promise."

CHAPTER TWENTY-SIX

La-di-da-da-dah, la-di-da-di-doh . . .

Dad thrums the steering wheel in time to the country waltz playing on the radio as we drive home from the stable. I slump sullenly next to him, frozen in the passenger seat.

"You all set for the invitational?" he asks cheerily. "Did you show the other kids your new jacket? And the patch?"

Ummm . . . does he not see the tears still trickling down my cheeks?

"No, I did *not* show them my new jacket, Dad," I snap. "Because I quit the team."

"Whoa, whoa, whoa." He looks over and finally notices the damp streaks under my eyes. "What happened, Wills? Why are you crying?"

"Clyde has OCD!" I blurt.

"Oh gosh, hon," he says, frowning. "I didn't know horses got OCD . . ."

"It's a different kind of OCD—bone cysts," I explain, wiping my damp face on the back of my sleeve. "Nobody can ever ride him again unless he gets a surgery. But Georgia says she can't afford the surgery. *Or* Clyde's boarding fees. So after the invitational, she's putting him up for auction."

"Oof. I'm so sorry, kiddo." He passes me a packet of Kleenex from the console.

"There just *has* to be a way to get Clyde the operation, Dad. Or at the very least, keep him at Oakwood," I say before blowing my nose.

"You know how much I wish we could make that happen, Wills. But those boarding fees—let alone the surgery—are way, *way* out of our budget. That's why we've only been borrowing Clyde for your lessons."

"They want to ship him off somewhere he can supposedly 'rest quietly,'" I say, adding sarcastic air quotes.

"Resting quietly sounds like a pretty good deal to me." Dad chuckles to himself as he turns onto our block.

"But he doesn't want to *rest quietly*," I insist, my frustration bubbling over. "Why do grown-ups think everyone wants to rest quietly? Clyde loves Oakwood—it's been his home for years and years. And the surgery could completely heal him if it works!"

"That's a big *if*, Wills."

"Well, *if* Clyde can't stay at Oakwood, then I don't want to be on the Oakwood team." I cross my arms across my chest defiantly.

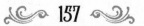

My dad clears his throat. "Wills, I know you're upset right now."

I sniffle and brace myself for a pep talk that I am *not* in the mood for.

"But you're behaving like an immature, whiny, selfish . . . brat."

Wait—what? I whip my head around. I was expecting a little sympathy and encouragement from my dad, not a sick burn! He turns the car into our driveway, but stops short before pulling into the garage.

"All those kids on the Oakwood Flyers are counting on you for that horse show this weekend. Do you plan on letting them all down?" He turns his shoulders so they're squared with mine. "And what about me and your mom? We had a deal about you making an effort. I made you pancakes twice in one week! Now you're going back on your word to us?"

"I . . ."

"That's not how this family operates," he says sternly. "We're not quitters." Then he pauses before adding the stinger. "Do you think Clyde would be proud of the way you're acting right now?"

I look down to my lap and shake my head slowly.

"I know how much that horse means to you, Wills. I wish I could wave a magic wand and get the money so he could stay here forever. But quitting the team isn't going to solve anything—for you or for Clyde."

More tears streak down my cheeks. My dad rolls the car

into the garage and climbs out of the driver's seat.

"You said Georgia isn't going to put Clyde up for sale until *after* the invitational, right?" he asks, grabbing his coat from the seat.

I nod, still staring at my lap and blubbering.

"Well, I'd say that gives you three more days to figure out a miracle." He pats my shoulder as his eyes crinkle into a smile. "Assuming you can stop feeling sorry for yourself for a few hours?"

I look up and manage a sniffly smile in return. "I'll try."

"Thatta girl."

As he walks into the house, I bolt up in my seat with a realization. Dad is right! If nobody else can save Clyde . . . I'll just have to save him myself.

CHAPTER TWENTY-SEVEN

"And that's why, after thousands of years, Arabians remain the most valiant and endurant of horse breeds, beloved by riders around the globe."

Kay slow-claps as I finish reading my English presentation in the kitchen and take a bow.

"Not exactly scintillating content, but I give you an A-plus for enthusiasm," she says. "I can't believe your teacher is letting you do *another* project on Arabian horses."

"It's the *same* project," I correct her. "It was a serious, six-month research assignment. But honestly? I could have spent my entire life on it."

"Cool. Can we go back to *silent* study time now?"

"So nice to see my girls supporting each other!" Dad says as he slides piles of waffles onto our plates. "Remember, Kay's in charge while I'm away on my work trip. Mrs. Kochenderfer is right next door if you need anything."

"I think we got it the first eighteen times you explained it, Dad," Kay says, meticulously measuring a single drop of syrup into each of her waffle squares.

"Wills, I already texted Georgia to let her know that you'll be competing with the team, despite your little outburst yesterday. The matter is *not* up for discussion."

"Sounds good—thanks, Dad!" I say chipperly, flooding my plate with a tsunami of syrup.

He looks up, surprised. "Huh, I wasn't expecting that to go so well. I guess my little tough-love speech in the car worked?"

"Mmmm-hmm," I say, jamming a forkful of waffle in my mouth.

"I'm glad to hear it," he says, grinning sheepishly. "Because I was *really* out of my comfort zone there."

And it *did* work. My dad said I need to come up with a miracle for Clyde—and that's exactly what I plan to do. I just need to keep the details of said miracle (aka MISSION: CLYDE) top secret for the time being.

"Okay, then!" Dad continues, pleased with himself. "I'll leave the Oakwood entrance fee in an envelope on the counter. And extra money for emergencies."

"What about extra money for pizza?" Kay asks.

"Pizza definitely qualifies as an emergency!" I add quickly, syrup dribbling down the corner of my mouth.

"I'll leave plenty of money for food as well," he says. "Wills, don't forget to polish your boots before Saturday. You've got to pass inspection—just like Mom taught you."

He slides a tin of polish and a shoe brush across the table as we gobble down the rest of our waffles. "The boots," he adds, clearing his throat, "which I hope you are not wearing inside the house right now."

"Of course not!" I scramble to tug off the muddy culprits under the tablecloth.

He shakes his head, but I catch a subtle grin lifting the corners of his mouth. "Okay, let's go through the schedule one more time. Friday after school Kay takes you to groom Minnie, then Saturday morning it's Kay's quiz bowling—"

"Quiz *bowl*," she corrects him.

"—followed by Wills's horse showing."

"Horse *show*." I giggle. (He's just trolling us now.)

"We get it, Dad!" Kay sighs.

"All right, all right—I'll handle the dishes tonight." He smiles, swooping our plates to the sink. "You two get your homework done and a good night's sleep—you have a big weekend of independence ahead of you, young ladies!"

Kay and I both cringe at his cheesiness.

"Good luck at your meeting, Dad," Kay says as we both hug him good night. "Don't worry, Wills will probably only burn down *half* the house while you're gone."

CHAPTER TWENTY-EIGHT

Eeeee-oooooo-eeeeee-oooooo!

Someone call a fire engine, because my big final Arabian horse presentation during first-period English was lit! (My teacher called it "ahem, extremely thorough, Wills"—boom!)

Now I just have to suffer through the rest of the school day. I count down the seconds as the clock creeeeeps sooooo slooooowly. I struggle to remember the Continental Congress in second period or the difference between igneous and sedimentary rocks in third period or how to balance complex equations in fifth. All I can focus on is how anxious-excited-nervous-giddy I am about the invitational—not to mention my top secret plan to save Clyde!

After school, Kay follows Dad's orders, dropping me off at Oakwood so that I can get Minnie glamorous before the big show tomorrow. Kay is *not* pleased that she has to wait in the car on a Friday night while I groom my horse. But I'm

not pleased that I have to get up early and sit through her Knowledge Maestros competition in the morning. So we are equally *not* pleased.

See? I'm getting better at balancing complex equations!

"You have two hours, tops," Kay warns me as she ever so slowly guides Mom's SUV into a parking spot. Kay has had her license for only a few months and is terrified of making a mistake, so her preferred driving speed is "slower than an elderly tortoise."

"Pick me up at the back entrance, okay?"

"Fine. But I need to study for quiz bowl tonight. So if you're not in the car by six p.m., you'll have to find a four-legged ride home."

"It would probably get me there faster!" I say, slamming the car door and running through the frigid February air into the stable.

As much as I'm eager to initiate MISSION: CLYDE, I decide to get Minnie groomed first so as not to raise any suspicions.

"Your stylist has arrived!" I whisper to Minnie, slipping a halter over her head.

She greets me with a snort, clearly disappointed that I'm carrying a grooming bucket instead of her food pail.

"Don't worry, Miss Minnie," I say, coaxing her out of the stall with an apple. "I promise you'll get your dinner just as soon as I'm done making you gorgeous."

I lead her to the shower stall in the barn, secure her

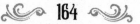

with crossties (safety first!), and give her a good bath with a sponge—keeping the water warm, since it's so chilly outside. I shampoo and condition her, working out the dirt and dust with a currycomb, then carefully rinse off all the suds. When we're done, I squeegee the excess water from her coat with a rubber scraper so she'll dry faster and spritz a detangling spray on her mane and tail.

I brush out her "bangs," deciding to leave her mane loose instead of braided—just in case, I might need something to grab on to if she gets feisty during the show tomorrow! Plus, braids take a ridiculously long time . . . time that I do not have with the MISSION: CLYDE clock ticking!

After brushing her mane, I run my hand gently along Minnie's back so she knows I'm heading toward her tail end. Trust me that you do *not* want to surprise a horse in its kicking zone, so I stand just off to the side as I comb out her tail.

I gather strands from her dock—the spot where her tail begins—and begin French-braiding the hair tightly. I weave her blond locks down a few inches, then let the bottom half of her tail flow freely. (Business in the dock, party in the back.)

Minnie lets out a pleased nicker, swishing her half-braided tail with approval.

"Work it!" I laugh.

Now this is teamwork!

I mist her coat with a shine spray, pull a blanket over her body to keep her warm and clean, and cover her legs with

stall wraps. This way she'll *supposedly* stay neat and tidy overnight. Finished![1]

"Just try not to swim in any mud puddles," I warn Minnie, giving her rump a pat and leading her back to her stall. As I start to walk away, Minnie cranes her head out to watch me, cocking her head curiously. "I'll see you tomorrow, girl," I call back to her, taking a big gulp. "It's going to be a big day for both of us."

As I walk down the hall, I check the time on my phone—eep, only twenty minutes to get my gear set before Kay leaves me to hitch-horse home! I scurry over to the tack room to quickly polish my saddle and bridle.

But as I struggle to pull Minnie's saddle down from the high hook, I hear the unmistakable giggles of Amara and the triplets floating in behind me. (Based on how happy Amara sounds, I'm guessing she hasn't spotted me.)

"Come on, let's do it now!" Amara says bossily.

"But what if she sees it before tomorrow?" Noel asks.

"Yeah, we don't want to ruin the surprise?" Everleigh adds.

---

[1] Before a show, you can cover your horse's legs in wraps or bandages to keep them fresh and clean—wraps can also help protect your horse's legs from scraping against fences or other injuries. Plus they look like adorable knee socks!

"I feel like she'll figure it out," Gwyneth says, concern creeping into her voice.

"Um, please?" Amara responds. "We'd have to spell it out on a T-shirt for her to figure it out."

Thwack!

Minnie's saddle tumbles to the floor, startling the four girls, whose faces turn as pale as a snow-white stallion. Amara quickly shoves her hands behind her back.

"Umm, can we *help* you?" she asks accusingly—as if I were trespassing in her personal tack room palace.

"I was just getting Minnie's saddle down to polish for the show tomorrow," I say, hoisting it onto the worktable and wiping it down with saddle soap. "What's the big surprise you guys were talking about?"

"Nothing!" they answer in unison.

"That's, like, basically the definition of a surprise?" Amara asks-slash-answers.

"It's not for you?" Everleigh blurts out.

"So you don't need to worry about it?" Noel whispers reassuringly.

"What are you doing here, anyway?" Amara asks, looking at me pointedly. "I thought you said you were quitting the team?"

"Oh," I mumble. "I only said that because I was really upset about Clyde. And the fact that Georgia might have to sell him."

Maybe I'm imagining things, but it looks like a flicker

of concern crosses Amara's face.

"I'm, uh, really sorry for taking it out on you, Amara," I continue. "I'm not quitting the team—I'll be there tomorrow."

"Lucky us!" Amara says brightly. (What I *thought* was concern on her face now looks suspiciously like a smirk.)

"If you'll still have me, that is?" I add sheepishly.

Gwyneth brightens. "Of course we'll still have you, Wills! The Flyers need you!"

"At least temporarily," Amara says, raising her gorgeous eyebrows. "So *don't* be late?"

She walks briskly out the tack room door. Everleigh, Noel, and Gwyneth follow quickly in her wake, like synchronized guppies.

But Gwyneth breaks away from the group and circles back to me. She smiles at me, her eyes dancing with excitement. "Tomorrow is going to be amazing!" And then, after glancing back over her shoulder to be safe, she lets out a little giggle and mimics Amara.

"So *don't* be late?"

CHAPTER TWENTY-NINE

Ba-da-da-bum-ba-da-ba, bum-ba-da-ba, bum-bum-da-buuuum!

The alarm clock on my phone sounds exactly like a bugle call at a horse race. That's my five-minute warning to get *out* of the barn and back into the car. Before Kay turns into an angry pumpkin.

I hastily buff the polish off Minnie's saddle and hoist it back on its rack (her bridle will have to wait until tomorrow). I toss my grooming bucket in my cubby and make a mad dash for Clyde's stall.

"Pfffffttttttttt!"

"I'm sorry, boy. I didn't forget you."

He neighs at me grumpily.

"I just had to get Minnie groomed first . . . I sure wish I were getting *you* ready for the show."

Clyde turns his back to me so that I am now speaking to

his rump. Clearly he is not interested in excuses.

"Hang on a minute." I grin. "You haven't heard my genius plan to save you yet!"

I walk around to his front side and untie his lead. "If you can't stay here at Oakwood, you're just going to have to come stay with me."

I lean into his chest, attempting to back him up out of the stall, but (surprise, surprise) he won't budge.

"Clyde, of all the times to choose to be difficult, this is *not* the moment."

Fortunately, I came prepared. I reach my hand in my pocket and pull out my secret weapon: a miniature candy cane. It's Clyde's favorite treat in the history of treats. His ears prick up at the sound of me unwrapping the crinkly plastic packet, and he immediately pirouettes around, craning his neck toward my pocket.

"I thought a little snack might get your attention!" I giggle, presenting the minty treat flat on my palm. He scoops it up with his enormous lips and gobbles it down.

"Hurry, Clyde—we don't want to make Kay late for her quiz bowl study session." I lower my voice. "You wouldn't like Kay when she's late for her quiz bowl study session."

I shiver at the thought, then pick up Clyde's lead, walking him toward the stable's back entrance. He happily *clomp-clomp*s behind me. Now that he knows I have a candy cane stash, he'll follow me to the ends of the earth.

We slink out the back door of the stable and *clomp-clomp*

over the sidewalk toward Mom's car. But Kay's hypnotized by her phone and doesn't look up, even when I open the passenger door.

"You *barely* made it," she sighs, still staring at her screen and not noticing the giant horse standing behind me.

"Barely counts!" I say, leaning my face into the car. "But before we go, I need to ask you something important."

"The suspense is killing me," she deadpans, scrolling through her messages and not bothering to glance up.

"Do you think there's room in the back seat for Clyde?"

"Ha ha," she says, still glued to her screen. "Mom and Dad wouldn't even let us bring home a goldfish. Now get inside and close the door. It's *freezing*."

Clyde noses his giant black muzzle through the open door, straight toward Kay's ear.

"Pffffffttttttttt," he sniffs.

"AHHHHHH!" Kay screams, jumping three feet in her seat and dropping her phone on the floor. She glares at me with molten-lava eyes.

"ARE YOU TRYING TO GIVE ME A HEART ATTACK? Why is there AN OVERGROWN BARNYARD creature slobbering on me?" she yells.

"Because I'm bringing him home!" I explain. "Clyde and I can follow behind the car—it's not that far."

"Wills, are you *insane*?"

"I'm trying to save him!"

"How? By getting us all arrested for Grand Theft Equine?"

"It's not theft if they don't want him here," I argue. "And you *did* say that I should find my own four-legged ride home. So I, um, did?" I plaster a pretty-please-with-sugar-on-top smile across my face.

"Let me think about how to say this nicely," Kay begins softly, taking a deep breath. "In no universe of existence will I ever allow you to walk down a public street ON A HORSE THAT YOU STOLE WHILE I WAS BABYSITTING YOU!"

"You're not baby—"

She holds up a hand, stopping me. "Dad will *murder* me if I let you bring a horse in the house."

"It's only temporary!" I protest. "And I'm not a *child*—I know I can't keep a horse in my room. Although that idea does sound amazing. But I promise, it's just for one night until I can figure out a better plan. I'll keep him in the garage!"

"You will keep him in his *pen*, where he belongs!"

"It's not a pen, it's a stall!"

"Is that really the point you want to argue at this moment?"

Clyde and I both try our best to look pitiful. "Please, Kay? Clyde means everything in the world to me. I can't let Georgia just auction him off to some stranger—what if he ends up as dog food?"

Clyde swishes his tail nervously and stamps a foot. A flicker of sympathy flashes across Kay's face.

"Listen, Wills. If you try to walk Clyde all the way home,

you could make his injuries worse." She lets out a sigh. "You don't want to hurt him, do you? Now, please. Take him back inside the stable where he's safe, okay? Before we all land in horse jail."

My shoulders slump in defeat as I reluctantly return Clyde to his stall. As upset as I am that my MISSION: CLYDE was foiled, I would never want to hurt Clyde. So I hurry back to the car and click on my seat belt—Kay's wrath for making her late for studying is not something I am prepared to toy with at this juncture of my existence.

"You're kind of obsessed with finding a way to keep Clyde around, aren't you?" she says, as she inches her way toward home.

"*Kind of* is an understatement," I sigh.

She flicks on the blinker (about two miles before our street). "Instead of horse-napping him, why don't you just raise the money to pay for his boarding fees at the stable?"

I light up. Why hadn't I thought of this?

"That's a great idea, Kay! I could make some of Mom's famous peanut-butter fudge tonight. And I could sell it at the horse show tomorrow!"

"Wait, how much money do you need exactly?" she asks, crunching over a pile of slush as she slowly turns onto our street, pausing for nonexistent traffic.

"Hmmm, to pay his boarding fees for the entire year, I'd need to sell . . ." I attempt to work out the algebra in my head. "Roughly five thousand squares of fudge by tomorrow."

"Don't forget to factor in the cost of ingredients," Kay adds helpfully.

Fudge! There's no way I can balance that equation by tomorrow. Which means my MISSION: CLYDE 2.0 has failed before it even began. (And before I even got to nibble on a single bite of fudge. Blergh.)

Kay creeeeeeeps the car into the garage. When she finally puts the gear into park, I leap out of the passenger seat. I now have less than twenty-four hours to survive the invitational and come up with a new, foolproof MISSION: CLYDE 3.0. I have no time to waste!

Just as soon as I eat dinner . . .

CHAPTER THIRTY

"I'm *huuuungry*," I whine to Kay. "Where's the pepperoni I was promised?"

Friday night means pizza-for-dinner, which Kay and I love *almost* as much as Wednesday breakfast-for-dinner. Friday also means no homework for me, which means I can devote myself *entirely* to prepping for the invitational tomorrow—and coming up with a new genius scheme to save Clyde.

After Kay orders the pizza, she devotes herself *entirely* to memorizing the moons of Jupiter, the maharajas of India, the suffragettes who chained themselves to railings to fight for women's right to vote, the doomed wives of Henry VIII, and whatever other random facts she'll need for her Knowledge Maestros trivia competition tomorrow.

All her studying suddenly gives me a brilliant idea.

"Call me when the pizza's here!" I shout as I hurry into the garage to gather the supplies I'll need to pull off my new, top secret MISSION CLYDE: 3.0.

I open the trunk of the car and shove all the secret gear into the wayback—along with my riding helmet, so I won't forget it in the morning. But as I fling my helmet, a folded note flutters out. And it's got a purple *W* on the front, just like all the rest!

Hmmm, someone must have slipped it into my helmet while I was grooming Minnie earlier at the stable—but who?

I quickly unfold the note, hoping this time I might finally solve the mystery . . .

Dear W,

Have you guessed who I am? Do you already know?
All will be revealed at our big show.
You'll find me in the Valiant place
And get to the bottom of this wild horse chase.

—A friend

Whoa. All will be revealed! At the big show! Which is tomorrow!

But where's this so-called Valiant place? Is that a secret spot at Oakwood that I don't know about? Am I supposed to ask for directions? ("Excuse me, Amara, can you direct me to the Valiant place?") Everyone at the stable would look at me like I'm a bigger weirdo than I already am. Blergh! I am no closer to solving this mystery than I was on day one. And all this sleuthing is making me hangry . . .

I hurry inside from the garage into the kitchen. But there's still no pizza. Pepperoni blergh!

Since I still have no hope of solving my friend mystery (at least until tomorrow), I focus on getting myself ready for the show. I want my turnout (all my clothes and gear) to be absolutely perfect for the invitational. Georgia says that being neat and clean and freshly pressed is a serious sign to the judges that you're serious about being a serious rider.

Or, as Amara likes to drill into all the Oakwood Flyers: "Dress well, test well!"

I start with my boots—buffing, polishing, and shining until they gleam so brightly I can practically see my braces shining back at me. I place the boots carefully next to the garage door so I won't forget to bring them in the morning.

Then I dash up to my room to retrieve my new (or should

I say, Luis Valdez's old!) riding jacket. I fling open the closet door and find it hanging right in the center, its brass buttons still shining brightly. And phew . . . Dad remembered to sew on Mom's golden-wing patch before he left for Chicago. It's floating regally on the left side of the coat, just beneath the elegant notched collar.

Okay, so it looks like Dad actually *stapled* the wings on. But as he likes to say: "I won't tell Martha Stewart if you won't."

Now it's time to iron my white collared shirt and breeches so I look like a serious #HorseGirl. I turn back to my closet to grab the shirt, but I don't see it hanging in my "fancy clothes" section (which is, in reality, two hangers).

I flip through those two "fancy" hangers again and again— and even expand the search to the "not fancy" section of the closet. I scour the "outgrew it but not ready to say goodbye" section in the way back of the closet, but the shirt is nowhere to be found. Blergh!

In desperation, I drop down to my pile of "let's see if they still smell tomorrow" clothes on the floor, pinching my nose closed as I rummage through the mountain of stinky horse-themed tops and gym clothes.

"Aha!" I bravely plunge my arm into the pile of stench. There, hiding at the very bottom, is the missing white button-down.

Of course! I wore it back in October for my Amelia Earhart costume at the Halloween parade! It must have somehow

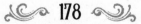

disappeared in my Bermuda Triangle of laundry . . . for three months. Yikes.

I pluck the shirt from the bottom of the pile, give it a sniff (then immediately regret giving it a sniff), and toss it in my laundry basket. Now where in the heck are my breeches?

I search my dresser, the closet, and various clean/dirty/ toxic-danger-zone laundry piles. I empty drawers, tossing clothes left and right, but find zero pairs of breeches.

Oh no, this is bad. I *cannot* go to my first horse show without pants . . .

CHAPTER THIRTY-ONE

Click click click.

Kay has already told me twice that under no circumstance whatsoever can I interrupt her again tonight while she's prepping for Knowledge Maestros. So I do the only thing I can think of. I pick up the phone and furiously tap out a text to Mom.

> HELP!!!!

It takes Mom only a few seconds to respond.

> Sweetheart, what's wrong? Did you call 911?

> My breeches are missing! And I need them for the invitational tomorrow!!

As I wait for Mom to write back, I tear around my room in a frenzy, pulling open old gym bags, leafing through my filing cabinet, and even checking the Breyers shelf above my bed, all in a desperate search for my pants. When I finally hear my phone chime, I'm out of breath.

Are you by any chance wearing them? 😕

I look down. *Oops.* I am indeed wearing said breeches— I forgot I put them on this morning, in order to add "authenticity" to my Arabian horse final presentation in English class.

Oh yeah, I guess I am. 🙁

How did you know??

Call it mother's intuition. 👩

Oops?? 🙁🙁

Willa, you are never to send an emergency text about LAUNDRY again!!

You nearly gave me a heart attack! 💚🐴👍

OK. Sorry. Can we FaceTime later?

I wish, sweetheart, but I'm on duty at zero-dark-thirty.

Good luck tomorrow, baby!

> Fly high . . . and don't break a leg!

> 🚫👢

I'm dying to ask Mom for some advice on MISSION: CLYDE 3.0, but my gut tells me she'll just try to stop me from my plan. (That could also be my gut telling me it wants pizza.) But to be safe, I just tap out:

> Thanks, Mama. Wish you were here. 🙁🖤

After I dash off the text, I fling my phone on the bed in frustration. And then it hits me . . . the reason Mom can't FaceTime. The reason Dad is out of town. The reason they both insisted I couldn't quit the team:

MOM IS COMING HOME TO SURPRISE ME AT THE INVITATIONAL! DAD IS PROBABLY DRIVING TO PICK HER UP AS WE SPEAK!

It's exactly what happens in the zillions of YouTube videos I've watched of military parents coming home to surprise their kids. I know exactly how it will go down. I'll be competing in my equitation class and Mom will be hiding in the crowd and then she'll leap up and hug me and I'll cry and she'll cry and everyone will cry, probably even the horses.

And everything will finally, *finally* make sense again.

OMG, why didn't I think of this sooner?

But I can't let Mom know that I know. No, not after she's gone to all this trouble to surprise me. And I can't tell Kay, either—I'm dying see the look on her face when Mom pops out of the crowd. Eeeep!

I giggle giddily to myself, imagining it all. The video of our reunion is probably going to be watched by zillions of people around the world. I blush at the idea, then slip on my new riding jacket and practice looking surprised in the mirror.

I stare at my reflection, turning this way and that, miming a shocked expression . . . then stunned . . . then OMG-I'm-ugly-crying. My crocodile tears suddenly feel real.

I reach into my jacket pocket for a tissue—I'll need to practice elegantly dabbing tears from my eyes for the camera—when my fingers stumble on a hard cylinder. I reach in deeper and fish out . . . a purple pen.

A purple pen. From Luis Valdez's jacket.

A PURPLE PEN . . . FROM LUIS VALDEZ'S JACKET!

Luis must have forgotten the purple pen in the jacket when he left it in the lost and found. No, no, noooooo—he probably *gave* the jacket to Georgia to give to me as a secret surprise—and then left the pen inside as another clue. OMG, that has to be it!

In an instant, the rest of the puzzle solves itself. The note said I would find my friend in the *Valiant* place. And as I learned from my (ahem, *amazingly thorough*) Arabian horse essay, "valiant" means "displaying bravery . . . or valor." And "valor" is just one letter away from "Valdor"—Luis's horse! The Valiant place must be Valdor's stall!

I pull out the suspect list from under Secretariat's foot to be sure.

The only names left are Amara and Luis. And Amara is *definitely* not A friend. So the purple pen proves it once and for all . . .

OAKWOOD FRIEND SUSPECTS

~~GWYNETH~~
~~EVERLEIGH~~
~~NOEL~~
AMARA
~~GRAY~~
LUIS
~~GEORGIA~~
~~DAD~~
~~KAY~~
~~DR. MANSFORD~~

Luis Valdez is my friend! O! M! Geeeeee!

My dimples ripen to what must be cherry red as I lift Secretariat from my Breyers shelf and dance deliriously around the room with him. I'm dying to call Mom or Gwyneth or Clyde so I can tell another human being (or *horse* being) this thrilling news.

But I know that I can't.

The note was *very* clear about that.

All will be revealed at our big show.

I'm supposed to find my "friend" (aka Luis, aka OMG!) at the Valiant place tomorrow. I can't tip off anyone else to the big secret before then. If Luis and I are going to be friends, I should really respect his wishes, right? Isn't that what friends do for each other?

I'm not sure! I haven't really had any human friends before!

SO MUCH IS HAPPENING!

Before I hyperventilate, I take a deep breath, stable Secretariat back on his shelf, then focus on putting the final touches on my outfit for tomorrow. I shimmy out of my breeches and toss them in the laundry basket with my stinky white shirt. I pull on some pj bottoms and carry the entire basket of filthy clothes to the hallway, then dump everything down the chute.

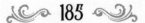

"Pizzaaaaaaaa!" Kay's voice calls up from the laundry room below—just in time for my filthy clothes to tumble straight into her face.

Oops?

As Kay squeals (and sneezes) in horror, I softly close the laundry chute and wait a few seconds for her "dander sensitivity" to die down. I hear her grumbling in the kitchen as she washes the "horse" off her face. Which gives me time to tiptoe down to the laundry room without having to deal with her sneeze-fueled wrath.

I fling open the washing machine lid and quickly shovel in all my clothes. I notice a pile of Kay's sweatshirts lying haphazardly on top of the dryer and decide to throw them in the washer, too.

See? I can be a thoughtful and caring sister when I want to be.

Plus, I know Kay will want to look her best tomorrow when she's on camera hugging Mom. I smile to myself, imagining the whole scene, as I pour in a cup of electric-blue detergent in the washer and flick it on.

After I'm done, I saunter into the kitchen, still wearing Luis's riding jacket (I am *so* not taking it off for the rest of time) over my pj bottoms. Kay, in turn, is still scowling over the surprise attack of dirty laundry. But the heavenly aroma of mozzarella and tomato sauce wafting from the cardboard box on the counter seems to have temporarily soothed her fury.

"You sure you want to wear your new fancy jacket while we're eating pepperoni?" she asks, flipping open the pizza box. The steam from its golden dough fogs her cat-eye glasses.

"You sure you want to wear your fancy glasses while we're eating pepperoni?" I retort. "But, uh, good point."

As she wipes her glasses clean with a flimsy paper napkin, I bound back upstairs to my room and hang the jacket carefully on my bedroom doorknob so there's no way I'll forget it in the morning. Then I run back downstairs, slap a slice of greasy pizza onto a paper plate, and dig in.

"We're leaving the house at seven a.m. tomorrow," Kay announces bossily. "Sharp."

"But your trivia thing doesn't start until nine," I protest, my mouth full of gooey cheese.

"Well, I'm the driver. So I say when we leave. And I like to be there fifteen prior to fifteen prior—just like Mom."[1] Kay carefully slices a bite of pizza with her fork and knife. "It helps psych out the competition."

I know better than to argue, so I just roll my eyes. The eye-roll volley continues for a while, before Kay gives up and returns to her quiz bowl questions.

"Fun fact," I muse out loud after a beat of silence. "Most

---

[1]   Mom has a rule that we should be ready to go "fifteen minutes prior to fifteen prior"—that's military speak (aka Mom speak) for being not just *on time* to something, but early. The idea is that you should get there "fifteen minutes prior" to your boss, who is supposed to get there fifteen minutes before her boss, etc. Kay, of course, believes that she is my boss and that I should always be ready fifteen minutes prior to her. Blergh.

Arabian horses have five back vertebrae instead of six like other horses."

"Wills, I told you I'm trying to concentrate!"

"I was just trying to help you with some trivia!"

"I highly doubt Knowledge Maestros has a barnyard category. And even if it did—"

Buzzzz. Saved by the washer. I dash to the laundry room and toss the wet clothes into the dryer. I don't want to take any chances with damp clothes in the morning, so I turn the dial to HOT/EXTRA DRY and hit start.

Then it's back upstairs to escape Kay's silent study zone. I scoop Secretariat from the shelf above my bed and go over all my big plans for the morning—winning a ribbon at the invitational, "friending" with Luis, saving Clyde, and hugging Mom. (!!!!)

I don't know how I'll possibly fall asleep in a million years. *Zzzzzzzzzzzz.*

CHAPTER THIRTY-TWO

Beep beep, beep beep, beep beep.

My alarm startles me awake at the crack of 6:00 a.m. the next morning. I wipe the sleep from my eyes and bolt upright in my bed.

It's the day of the show! 🐎🐎🐎🐎🐎🐎

After the world's fastest shower, I bundle myself into my robe, snatch Luis's riding jacket (swoon!) from the doorknob, where I carefully left it the night before. Then I scamper down to the laundry room and yank open the dryer door. Kay's mountain of school sweatshirts tumbles out, along with my breeches. But I can't find my white button-down anywhere in the pile.

I sift through the sweatshirts again, tossing them haphazardly in the laundry basket. Still no white shirt. I reach my hand deep into the far corner of the dryer and pull out the only thing that's left, a purple tie-dyed shirt.

Huh, I don't remember Kay having any purple tie-dyed shirts . . .

Oh no. Oh no, oh no, oh *nooooo*.

The purple pen must have fallen out of Luis's jacket pocket while I was putting the clothes in the washer last night! And then exploded in the dryer! All over my white button-down! Which also seems to be several sizes smaller than it was last night.

Did I mention this is *not* good? *Oh noooooooooo!*

"Fifteen minutes until the car leaves the driveway!" Kay yells from downstairs.

I fish the melted purple pen out of the dryer and stare at my shirt. Maybe nobody will notice that my wrists now stick out a good three inches from the end of the sleeves? Sleeves that are now splotched with giant purple stains?

I hear Amara's voice chiming in my brain: "Dress well, test well!"

Ugh, of *course* everyone will notice. *Especially* Amara. And the judges.

But I have no other option—I slip on the shirt and button it up, tugging my riding jacket over its shrunken purple glory. Then I yank on my breeches (which I realize are now also lavender) and socks, just as Kay flips open the laundry-chute door above me and calls down.

"Have you seen my Knowledge Maestros sweatshirt?"

Gulp.

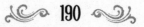

CHAPTER THIRTY-THREE

Squeeeeeeeak.

Kay and I sit silently in the car as the garage door cranks open. She's wearing her shrunken and purple-splashed Knowledge Maestros sweatshirt. I'm wearing my shrunken and purple-splashed button-down and breeches.

"Well, at least we got all the bad luck out of our system early!" I say, trying to sound cheerful as Kay glowers from behind the steering wheel. "The day *has* to get better from here."

Crunch.

Kay rolls over something. It's my boots. Because of course I left them right behind the car so I wouldn't forget them in the morning. Mission accomplished!

"Okay, so it has to get better from *here*," I say as I run back to grab the scuffed and dented boots and tug them onto my feet.

CHAPTER THIRTY-FOUR

"You're welcome!" I singsong smugly to Kay as we pile back into the car after her trivia competition.

"Okay, okay." She grins, looking down at the trophy in her lap. "So it turns out knowing that Arabian horses have five vertebrae instead of six actually *did* come in handy."

"I told you!"

"Thanks, Wills, couldn't have done it without you," she says. "Or my sixteen years of studying."

I'm so relieved, I actually laugh.

"And now it's your turn to crush it," she says, putting the car in gear and driving—at a speedy fifteen miles per hour—toward Oakwood.

CHAPTER THIRTY-FIVE

"Beginner Novice jumpers, please report to the arena!" a voice booms over a loudspeaker.

When Kay and I finally arrive at Oakwood, the stable is already abuzz with horse trailers, horse parents, and, of course, #HorseGirls milling about in their jackets and jodhpurs.

More announcements echo from the indoor ring, followed by polite applause, as judges call out instructions for riders in the classes that have already begun to compete. The riders still waiting for their groups try to calm down their nervous horses (and themselves) with walks in the frigid outdoor warm-up ring.

Kay and I rush toward the "show office" (which is actually just the regular front desk of Oakwood, except draped with some colorful bunting in honor of the big day) so I can register.

"You made it, Miss Willa!" Georgia says. "I was beginning to worry." She eyes my purple-splattered button-down, then shifts her gaze to Kay's purple-splattered sweatshirt. "I'm gonna go ahead and guess you two are sisters?"

Kay and I nod sheepishly.

"It's my fault," I explain. "I had a laundry emergency."

"Happens to the best of us," Georgia answers briskly, waving away my worries.

"Here's Wills's entrance fee," Kay says, handing over the envelope Dad left. "And the permission slip for me to be her 'adult' for the day."

"You make an excellent adult," Georgia says as Kay beams. "Now, Wills, let's get you signed up for the Walk-Trot-Canter Equitation class. It starts at two o'clock sharp, but you still need to get Minnie tacked up and warmed up. No time to waste!"

Georgia hands me my competition number—80—which Kay pins carefully to the back of my jacket. She also hands me a smaller number to pin to Minnie's bridle.

"Are you nervous?" Kay asks.

I wipe the sweat from my clammy palms onto my lavender breeches. "Why do you ask?"

"No reason!" She smirks.

A fat drop of sweat slides down my forehead and lands—*splat*—on her perfect white sneakers. But instead of freaking out about having "horse" dripped on her, she wraps me in a giant hug.

"You're going to do great," she reassures me. "I'll be right over there, cheering you on from the stands."

"That's what I'm afraid of," I joke, smiling up at her gratefully. If only I could tell her that Mom will also be cheering me on from the stands. I still have to keep all my secrets secret for just a tiny bit longer.

As Kay walks toward the bleachers, I head to Clyde's stall for a preshow good-luck nuzzle. He *pfffffftttttttttt*s softly, resigned to the fact he won't get to compete with all the other horses.

"I know, Clyde," I say. "I wish I were riding you, too. But I'll be right back after the show, I promise. Don't worry, I've come up with a brand-new MISSION: CLYDE 3.0 to save you!"

I glance out in the barn aisle to make sure no one's watching, then casually stash my top secret supplies behind the hay bales stacked just outside his stall.

"Nobody's taking you anywhere, boy," I say firmly, patting his flank. "At least not without me."

I close his stall door gently, then hurry over to Minnie. She greets me with a cheerful neigh and a stamp of the foot, pushing her face over her door as if to hurry me along. She can feel the electricity of the invitational pulsing through Oakwood, and she does *not* want to be left out of the party.

"Sorry I was late," I say, tacking her up as quickly as I can (which is not very quickly at all, considering my nerves have made me even clumsier than usual). "But I had a top secret

195

mission to handle! I'll tell you all about it after the show."

After she's saddled up, I loosen the knots from her crossties, pull the bridle reins over her neck, and slide the bit into her mouth. Then I pin our number 80 to her bridle.

"Voilà, you're ready!"

Minnie tosses her mane cheekily.

I lead her to the warm-up ring (also known as a schooling ring) and mount up with ease. The arena is bustling with riders from all the major stables in the region; Minnie and I have to stay alert so we don't get in anyone's way.

"All we have to do is walk, trot, and canter," I repeat to her, trying (and failing) to sound confident. "We've done that a million times. Now we just have to do it in front of a judge. So there's absolutely no need to be nervous!"

More sweat pours down my forehead (and—yep, the faucet's open—my armpits) as I notice Amara and Silver Streak trotting into the practice ring.

Amara's hair is twisted tightly into two braids, with bedazzled blue ribbons waving out from the ends (of *course* Amara would award herself two blue ribbons before the show even begins). Her boots are pristine; her shirt is so white, it practically glows. Silver Streak's mane, meanwhile, has been woven into a parade of tidy button braids.[1]

---

1   Button braids are a fancy way to style a mane—they look like a parade of perfect buttons marching down your horse's neck. But they take yarn, needles, and tons of time and patience to perfect. Obviously I'm sticking with an unbraided mane for Minnie.

 196

The other Oakwood Flyers huddle around Amara for a team meeting. The girls are all kitted out in beautiful ribbons and finery, while the boys look shockingly clean. I hang back a bit from the group, hoping that Amara won't notice my purple tie-dyed shirt. But Minnie betrays me, trotting me right over to the center of the action.

"You're *late*?" Amara scolds me. And then her gaze lands on my clothes. "Well, that's definitely . . . a look?"

"I accidentally made it myself," I mutter.

"Don't worry," she sighs. "Since you're only riding in the equitation class, the judges won't take off points for appearance. Just try not to trip during all that complicated *walking* and *trotting*?"

"And *cantering*!" I add brightly.

"You're going to do great, Wills!" Gwyneth calls to me, offering me a reassuring grin.

"Just try not to look so nervous?" Noel adds with a look of concern that is definitely *not* reassuring.

"Why does everyone think I'm nervous?"

"Probably because you're dripping purple sweat?" Everleigh answers helpfully.

I wipe a jacket sleeve across my forehead, attempting to dab up the lavender lagoon.

"Speaking of nerves, how are you feeling today, Amara?" Gwyneth asks tentatively.

"Like a winner!" she says a bit too quickly, pressing her lips into a tight smile. "I'm completely relaaah—" But before

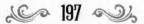

she can finish her sentence, a tiny burp escapes her mouth, startling all of us (and our horses).

Panic dances in Amara's eyes as she claps a hand over her mouth. "It's just hiccups!" she says defensively, even though nobody asked. "They're good luck?"

Luis doesn't seem convinced. "Your, uh, tummy good?"

Gray leans in eagerly. "Did you drink any of that orange electrolyte stuff again?"

The rest of us hold our breaths, waiting for Amara's answer.

"Of *course* not," she snaps, her eyes narrowing as she scans the circle of Oakwood Flyers with her Stare o' Death. "I didn't drink anything at all. For the last twelve hours. Because I'm perfectly fine. And in control. And whatever happened last year is *definitely* not going to happen again. And I *thought* we weren't discussing it?"

I notice beads of sweat rolling down her otherwise pristine forehead. "Amara, are you sure you're feeling—?"

"Attention, Oakwood Flyers!" she announces, ignoring me entirely. "Everyone who's actually *jumping* today should get in one more set of practice fences.

"Those of you who are *not* . . ." She looks pointedly at me. "Maybe check a mirror to make sure you don't look like a giant grape?"

Her lips then curl into a bloodthirsty grin. "Now let's go *destroy* those Elkhorn Equestrians!"

Amara bounds off dramatically on Silver Streak. I may be

imagining things, but the other riders all seem to hang back a bit, not wanting to follow too closely in her splash zone.

As Luis glides past me, riding Valdor, I wave at them shyly. "Hi, friend!"

Luis turns, confused, and gives me a half wave back. "Um, hey?"

Ohhhhhh—I get it. Luis is still playing it cool until *after* the show, when we can finally confess our friendship for each other in private. He wouldn't want to make Amara or the other #HorseGirls jealous. That's how crazy thoughtful he is.

Swooooon!

As other riders leap over their practice jumps, Minnie and I walk steadily around the schooling ring. We accelerate into a trot, then a canter, then slow back down to a walk. Speeding up, then slowing down, over and over again. The entire time I try to keep my eyes up, my heels down, my shoulders back, my hands straight, and every other single one of Georgia's *brand-this-in-your-brain* rules I'm supposed to remember.

After several laps, I ask Minnie to halt, then I steal a glance around the ring. Amara is about to leap over a double combination. But a redheaded girl on a chestnut Hanoverian crosses in front of her.[2]

"Heads *up*?" the girl trills, smizing icily. "Move it or lose it, breeches!"

 2 Hanoverians are warm-blooded horses known for being calm, levelheaded, and naturally gifted athletes. (So basically the opposite of me!) They are famous for being some of the very best show jumpers in the world.

"That's Meghan Marscapone," Gwyneth whispers, sidling up to me on Molasses. "This *isn't* good."

"After you!" Amara smizes back at Meghan, yanking Silver Streak's reins and pivoting him out of the way.

Meghan soars confidently over the practice jump, clearing it by a mile, thanks to her horse's powerful hindquarters. Now it's Amara's turn.

"Good luck!" Meghan singsongs, glaring at Amara with sugary venom.

"I don't need any—" Amara coos back. But before she can finish her sentence, she lets out another burp, this one far bigger than the first.

She grimaces but refuses to slow down, jabbing Silver Streak in his sides and urging him on.

They circle around faster and faster, bounding toward the fence. Their tight braids gleam in the dazzling light as their bodies sail together in unison toward the jump. And only a few steps before they take off into the air, Amara breaks Georgia's *number four, most important, brand-this-in-your-brain* rule. Instead of looking ahead at the fence, she glances back at Meghan.

A look of pure terror flashes on Amara's face.

CHAPTER THIRTY-SIX

"Take cover!" Everleigh shouts, sounding the alarm.

"My baby!" Amara's mom calls, clambering down through the bleachers toward the schooling ring, her giant purse whacking other parents and children in her path.

"I can't believe this is happening again!?" Noel whispers.

Gray's mouth drops open. "It's like a slushie machine that won't turn off."

Luis nods, impressed.

"But I thought Amara didn't drink the orange electrolyte stuff this time," I whisper to Gwyneth.

"You don't know about the Incident *before* the Incident," Gwyneth whispers back to me. "It's not what she drinks, it's—"

"Everybody stay calm!" Georgia instructs, hustling to Amara's side and lifting her from the electric-green puddle at her feet. "You okay there, Captain?"

Amara screws her face into a furious scowl. "This is all *your* fault."

I steel myself. "Amara, I didn't . . ." But before I can finish defending myself from an imaginary crime, I realize that Amara isn't looking at me. She's looking past me, toward her mother.

"Don't you worry, sweetheart," her mom says in a creepily bright voice, as if she's talking to a four-year-old. She pulls wet wipes out of her giant handbag and mops down Amara's chin. "You're going to have an *amazing* career as a show jumper. I promise this will *never* happen to you again. We just need to find you a better horse. And a *much* better stable."

Georgia whistles softly. "You might want to find her some Pepto-Bismol first."

"Go *away*, Mom," Amara hisses. "Maybe I don't *want* an amazing career as a show jumper like you had. Maybe I just want to have fun—without all this pressure to be the perfect rider who wins everything."

"Sweetheart, don't say things you don't mean!" Her mom dabs at the green splashes on Amara's helmet. "You *are* going to win everything, just as soon as we get you the team you deserve."

Amara swats her hand away. "What I *deserve* is for you to not make me so nervous that my stomach experiences an exorcism during every big show."

Gwyneth turns to me. "Wills, we have a situation."

"I know," I whisper, nodding sympathetically to Amara. "I had no idea her mom put this much pressure on her to be perfect."

"Well that, too, but . . ." Gwyneth shakes her head. "Wills, there's no way Amara can compete now. We need you to take her spot in the jumper class."

I spin around. "You need me to do what?"

"We can't risk Amara puking again in front of the judges?" Noel agrees, striding over on Ginger.

"Yeah, that would be seriously not good," adds Luis, who's walked over on Valdor.

"I wouldn't mind watching Amara puke again!" Gray says excitedly from atop Bentley.

"No," Luis says firmly. "We can't let the Elkhorn Equestrians beat us again."

"Why can't one of you jump for Amara?" I ask, growing panicked. "Why does it have to be me?"

"Because the rest of us are already registered for our own jumper classes?" Everleigh explains from Cinnamon's saddle.

"And we don't have any other backup jumpers?" Noel points out.

I shake my head, unable to even imagine taking over for the Queen of the #HorseGirls.

"They're right," Amara groans, pushing past her mother and squishing her neon-green-splattered boots dangerously close to me and Minnie. "There's no way my stomach can handle jumping right now. And we need those points. Wills, you're our best—and to be clear—*only* option."

"Amara, look at me." I point to my purple-splattered shirt. "I can't even get my turnout right, let alone pull off a full show-jumping course! I'm not ready."

She stares back at me icily. "What you're not ready to do is to let your team down. I'll take your spot in the equitation class, since there won't be any jumps."

She winces as more gurgles erupt from her stomach. "Which means you've got to ride for me."

"But, I—"

"Sounds like a crackerjack plan!" Georgia says, walking over to me as Amara's mom scurries away to "find a supervisor."

My eyes plead with Georgia to save me from certain doom, but she insists on boosting my confidence instead. Blergh!

"Willa, you can do this. You've practiced all the jumps during lessons," she reminds me. "You even ran the full course a few times. And Minnie here"—Georgia gives Minnie's neck a scratch—"she knows exactly what to do."

"I . . . I . . . ," I sputter.

I think about Mom and what she said about being ready for the surprises in life. And what Dad said about being a good teammate. And what Georgia said about keeping hope in my heart. And what Kay said about . . . Well, I'm sure Kay said *something* encouraging at some point in my life.

"What do you say, Wills?" Gwyneth asks. "Are you in?"

I take a deep breath. "Okay." I swallow. "I'm in."

CHAPTER THIRTY-SEVEN

"Pffffft!"

This time it's me *pffffffft*-ing, instead of Clyde, as I try to calm myself down. By late afternoon, all the other Oakwood Flyers have finished competing in their various jumper divisions. And all of them scored spectacularly well. (No pressure!)

Amara swallowed her pride and—just as she promised—took my spot in the "baby" Walk-Trot-Canter equitation class, where she *(of course)* won first place and *(of course)* promptly rubbed it in the face of all the seven-year-old riders she was competing against. But at least the victory seemed to settle her stomach.

Thanks to Amara's first-place win, our team is now completely, exactly, officially tied with the Elkhorn Equestrians. And the only rider left to jump is . . . *gulp* . . . me.

I wipe down Minnie with a clean cloth, tuck my purple

tie-dyed shirt into my breeches, mount up, and wait for my turn in front of the judges. Everything seems surreally quiet—except for the sound of my heart beating way too fast.

I take a deep breath and mentally review the course in my mind. I walked through it earlier, making a careful plan for all the strides and angles I want to use for each fence and combination. Now if only I can remember the plan during my actual ride, and not fall on my—

"Rider number eighty!" a judge calls over the PA system. "Final call for rider number eighty?"

The crowd murmurs and glances around the room, searching for the missing equestrian.

"That's *you*, Wills!" Noel whispers, pointing to the 80 pinned on Minnie's halter. She and the other Flyers have gathered around me to wish me good luck. (Or, perhaps, watch me ruin everything they've been carefully working toward for years!)

"Here!" I say, startled out of my mental prep-slash-panic session.

"Are you nervous?" Everleigh asks again, squinting warily at me and Minnie.

"Of course not," I lie, wiping rivulets of lavender sweat from my forehead. "Why does everybody keep asking me that?"

"No reason," the team answers in unison. Maybe they're wondering if I've had any colorful energy drinks.

"You've got this, Wills." Gwyneth smiles brightly, patting Minnie's flank.

"Nothing you haven't done before," Luis adds in his deep, dreamy voice. *(Do not swoon. Do not swoon.)*

"Good luck," Amara says begrudgingly. "Just remember. We asked you to be an Oakwood Flyer for a reason?"

Whoa. Was Amara—Queen of the #HorseGirls—actually being *nice* to me? And encouraging? My jaw practically falls off my face.

Instead of playing it cool, I blubber with gratitude. "Thanks so much, Amara! It was, um, really nice of you to give me your spot, and to be so nice to me, and I really appreciate all the—"

"Just try not to fall?" she interrupts, whipping her braids around to gaze at Meghan Marscapone, who's beaming from the other side of the ring as the Elkhorn Equestrians congratulate her on jumping a clean course.

Oh, great! Meghan just finished the *entire* course without knocking over a single fence. Yes, she was a few seconds over the course time limit, which meant she did get one measly time fault. But otherwise? Perfection. Blergh!

I guess that this means that technically—in some alternative universe where I actually know what I'm doing AND ride the course perfectly with absolutely no mistakes AND finish under the time allowed—I could beat Meghan. Which means the Oakwood Flyers could win the invitational.

But of course we *don't* live in an alternative universe. We live in Nebraska. And I'm merely a beanstalk-tall #HorseGirl peasant, riding on a tiny pony.

"Next up, number eighty, Willa Watkins on Minnie."

I take a deep breath and say a silent prayer to the #HorseGods, hurrying Minnie into the ring while trying to stay relaxed and focused. I know the judges will be scrutinizing us from the moment we set hoof in the riding arena, so I need to attempt to look like I know what I'm doing. (Judges gonna judge!)

We trot around in what's called a courtesy circle—making a big loop in front of the judges as a sort of salute to them, which also lets them know we're ready to jump. As we finish the circle, I turn Minnie so that she's facing the first fence.

Our time won't start until we actually jump that first fence, but I open Minnie's stride up right away to set a strong pace.[1] Although her legs are shorter than any other horse in our group, she's happy to oblige, speeding up with giddy energy. Minnie clearly knows it's showtime—and she is ready to strut her stuff.

We canter toward the first jump—it's a vertical. I lean into a two-point position, and we have liftoff—Minnie leaps over the fence with confidence, clearing it easily, then sassily flicking her tail. I wish the judges gave extra points for flair!

We then make a tight loop toward the second jump—Minnie's hoof slides a bit on the hairpin turn. I get nervous

---

1   When horses get nervous, they sometimes take shorter strides. Opening up the stride means taking longer steps—which sets a faster pace. Of course this requires both the horse and rider to be relaxed and focused in the middle of a super-stressful competition. Easy!

that she might balk, but she recovers her footing and bounds toward the square oxer, its poles spread apart from each other.[2] This means Minnie's petite body has to leap as far across as a "normal" horse to clear the jump. But she sails over it like she's Big Ben. (Both the clock *and* the famous show-jumping horse.)[3]

"There you go!" Georgia cheers us on from the sidelines. "Nice!"

Minnie and I miraculously zip over several more obstacles without any faults. Before long, we're lining up for the final combination—a one-stride vertical followed by a four-stride bending line to the final fence, the tallest obstacle of the course. I remind myself to sit back in the saddle between the jumps and keep Minnie lined up as straight as possible.

"Okay, girl—we just have to make it over this last set without knocking over a fence," I whisper in her ear. "Or you know, tumbling to our doom!"

I worry Minnie might be growing tired, but her battery appears to be fully charged. A hush falls over the crowd as we canter toward the final combination.

---

2   A square oxer has two poles at the same height—but their height is the same as their width apart. (Thus the "square" thing.) This is pretty much the hardest type of oxer.

3   Named after that giant clock in England, Big Ben was one of the most famous show-jumping horses in history. He was 17.3 hands tall, and many people thought he was "too big to win"—but the gentle giant proved them wrong, getting first place in tons of jumping competitions and drawing huge crowds around the world. #GOALS!

Minnie makes it over the first vertical, then bounce-hops straight for the next fence. We skyrocket into the air toward the towering rail. But this fence looks like a mountain. I suddenly panic—I'm not sure if Minnie's little legs can make it all the way over.

Don't look down, don't look down, don't look down! I repeat to myself, invoking Georgia's *number four, most important, brand-this-in-your-brain* rule. *Look where you want to land!*

I will my chin—and Minnie—to stay up. And then everything starts to happen in slow motion. By some miracle, Minnie's front cupcake hooves make it over the jump with room to spare. But I hold my breath as the rest of her body arcs behind, her rear hooves hovering over the top rail by only a whisker!

Thud. We land solidly on the other side of the jump. As we canter away, I turn my head back to check the fence. Holy smokes—the rail stayed in place.

DID I MENTION WE LANDED? ON OUR FEET? *AND* THE RAIL STAYED IN PLACE?!

I think we just jumped clean.

"That's a clean ride for number eighty," a judge announces over the PA, confirming that my wildest dream did indeed actually just happen. I whirl my head and flick my eyes to check the clock on the judges' table.

Holy cow, we finished our ride under the time limit.

Which means I must have teleported to an alternative universe because Minnie and I JUST FINISHED A COMPLETELY CLEAN RIDE! No time penalties or refusals or faults or anything! WHAT'S THE OPPOSITE OF BLERGH?!

The other Oakwood Flyers go wild. (And by "go wild," I mean they clap really, really politely from the side of the ring.)

"Thatta *girl*!" Georgia grins, clapping slowly.

I circle Minnie around the ring to cool her down. My eyes, meanwhile, dart around, searching for Mom. I know she'll be popping up any moment to give me a giant congratulations hug.

But I don't see her curly hair and dimpled cheeks anywhere. And before I have time to find her face in the crowd, Georgia saunters over to me and Minnie. "Whoo-eee, Willa! That was a terrific ride! You and Minnie make one heck of a team."

I beam at her proudly.

"You better circle back around the ring, kiddo—it's almost time for the awards ceremony."

Of course! That's why I couldn't find Mom in the crowd. She's waiting until *after* the ribbon ceremony for her big reveal! She wouldn't want to steal my thunder before I get my blue ribbon—that is *so* like Mom.

"Thank you, Georgia!" I gush. "For your help and your

rules, and just . . . for everything."

Minnie and I trot giddily back to the center of the ring, where all the other riders from my group are waiting. By the end of the ceremony, when a judge clips the blue ribbon on Minnie's bridle, I'm so overwhelmed that I literally freeze with a giant smile baked onto my face.

Clyde would be so proud. Which of course makes me miss Clyde . . .

"WOO-HOO—that's my sister!" Kay shouts from the stands, standing up in her seat to whistle as everyone else around her applauds politely. "I mean—*woo-hoo*," she says quietly, slipping nonchalantly back into her seat.

I scan the bleachers, grinning wildly as I wait for Mom to appear. I look around the entire arena—twice—but I can't find her face anywhere. I slip my phone out of my pocket and text Kay.

> Have you seen her??

Who?

> Mom! She came back to surprise me!!! 🎉

?? Wills, you know Mom is on her base on the other side of the world, right? I just FT'd with her.

My grin collapses. I feel my heart literally sinking as I realize that this whole "big surprise" was all just a stupid, ridiculous fantasy in my mind.

Mom is, *of course*, still on the other side of the world. Dad is still in his stupid business meeting. And I'm still all alone here. Well, except for Kay, but that's only because I forced her to be here.

"Smile!" Amara mouths to me from the side of the ring, twirling her index fingers into her cheeks. "The Oakwood Flyers won! At least *try* to look like you're happy!?"

I plaster my fake smile back on, if only to stop myself from crying in front of the judges (or worse, Amara). Why do all my happys have to get mixed up with all my sads?

Which of course reminds me of the other giant sad in my life—Clyde. Georgia said she wouldn't put him up for auction until *after* the invitational. But the invitational is almost over. Which means that no matter how disappointed I am about Mom not being here, I don't have any time to waste . . .

"Your Intermediate Jumper class winner, Willa Watkins—representing the Oakwood Flyers—will now lead the riders in a victory lap around the ring."

At the judge's command, I force myself out of my haze of sadness and nudge Minnie ahead. She raises her petite head as high as it will go, trotting triumphantly around the arena as the Oakwood Flyers cheer for our champion lap.

Meghan Marscapone—with a scarlet-red, second-place ribbon pinned to her strapping Hanoverian—seems genuinely shocked to be following behind gangly me and tiny Minnie.

"Excuse me? Excuse me! Winners coming through!"

Amara asks-slash-chants, staring pointedly at Meghan. "Move it or lose it, breeches!"

Georgia shuts her down with a withering shake of the head. "Horsewomanship, Amara."

CHAPTER THIRTY-EIGHT

"Minnie, you were amazing!" I say, offering her a cool drink of water and a candy cane (or three) to devour back in her stall after the ribbon ceremony. I fling my arms around her chest. "I don't know what I would have done without you for the last few months while Clyde was sick."

She happily crunches away on the red-and-white-striped treats. I unbridle her, crosstie her, lift off her saddle, and give her a quick brush with the currycomb—all as fast as I possibly can.

"I'll be back soon to finish grooming you," I say, dropping the currycomb in my bucket.

Minnie stamps her feet.

"And to feed you dinner!" I laugh, brushing her mane out of her eyes. "I'm sorry I underestimated you, Minnie. You're a true champion—better than most horses twice your size. Now, if you'll excuse me . . . I have a secret mission to finish."

She swishes her tail, which I decide is her way of wishing me good luck.

I dash down to Clyde's stall and hug his giant neck. My heart wills my mom to pop out from behind him and hug *me*—but my brain reminds me that Mom secretly flying home to surprise me was all just a silly daydream. Mom isn't coming to rescue me. Or Clyde.

Which means I'm going to have to handle the rescuing myself.

With no time to mope, I get straight to work, feeding Clyde a candy cane and then digging through the pile of straw in the back corner of his stall while he munches away.

As I unbury my top secret supply bag, Clyde *pfffffftttttttt*s curiously, wondering why in the heck I'm pawing through a pile of straw. Instead of, you know, feeding him more pepperminty treats.

"Hang on, boy." I smile. "I'm here to save you!"

"Wills?" The low, movie-star voice floats in from the stable aisle.

I spin around and see two sets of large, dreamy eyes peering down at me from just outside Clyde's stall.

Oh no. *Oh no, oh no, oh no.* Luis Valdez and Valdor were *not* supposed to find me like this.

"What the . . . ?" Luis drops Valdor's lead and runs into

Clyde's stall, his eyes wide. "Wills, what happened? Are you okay?"

I follow his gaze to the long black cable of Kay's bicycle lock. Which I have wrapped tightly around my wrists. And then snaked around Clyde's giant neck. Looping us together in poly-coated braided steel.

"I'm totally fine," I say breezily, as if chaining myself to a horse were a completely normal thing to do. "Never been better!"

"Is this, like, a magic trick gone wrong?"

"Ha!" I say, trying to nonchalantly hide the bicycle cable behind my back but only managing to twist myself tighter in the cord. "You're *hilarious*, Luis."

The confused look remains firmly on his face.

"Speaking of hilarious," I continue with a nervous giggle. "This is all a really funny story. So Georgia told me she was going to put Clyde up for auction after the invitational. And I didn't want to lose my best friend. So I, um, decided to chain myself to him—ha!"

Luis frowns harder. "Wait, what?"

"I chained myself to Clyde," I say proudly. "This way, no matter what happens, we'll get to stay together. Forever!"

"Coooool," Luis exhales warily. "I, uh, just came by cuz Georgia wants to take a team photo."

"Coooool," I reply, oh-so-eloquently. I try to take a step toward him, then realize I can't move because . . . *I have chained myself to a horse.*

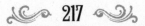

"Yeah, so I'm, uh—gonna go back out there," Luis says, turning to hurry Valdor down the stable aisle.

"Wait!" I cry.

Luis flips his head around in (I swear) slow motion. *Gulp.* I guess it's now or never.

"I know it was you."

CHAPTER THIRTY-NINE

"You know *what* was me?" Luis asks, pulling his boot back out of Valdor's stirrup and running a hand through his (glorious) hair.

"'Don't lose your *head*.' 'Meet me in the *Valiant* place.' Valiant, valor, *Valdor*." I point excitedly to Luis's horse before my chain yanks me back. "That was such a brilliant clue!"

He takes a cautious step backward. "You, uh, sure you're feeling okay, Wills?"

"I know you're A friend, Luis! I figured it out!" I flash him a giant, braces-filled grin.

Luis appears to be at a loss for words. *(Swoon!)* "I'm not sure I get what you're trying to say?"

"You can stop playing dumb." I roll my eyes playfully. "I found the purple pen in the pocket of this jacket. Which you 'pretended' to leave in the lost and found, knowing that Georgia would give it to me. And—"

"Hell-*oooo*?" interrupts a mesmerizing voice from down the stable aisle. "Wills? Luis? Everyone's looking for you—we're about to take the team photo?" Amara (of *course* it's Amara) pokes her head over Clyde's stall door.

But I keep my eyes locked on Luis. "You don't have to pretend anymore!" I plead desperately, grinning like a fool. "I know you wrote me those secret notes! See? The purple pen is in the jacket pocket. And your initials are on the jacket label!"

I struggle to slide the jacket off to show him, but it tangles in the bike lock.

Amara's mouth curls into an inscrutable smile. "May I?" she asks, sliding a manicured finger under my jacket collar and flipping the tag up before I can protest.

She raises an eyebrow at Luis. "It *does* say 'LV'?"

"Exactly!" I squeal triumphantly. "LV . . . Luis Valdez!"

Luis shakes his head. "But, uh, that's not my jacket."

Amara, meanwhile, dissolves into a fit of giggles. "Of course it isn't! 'LV' isn't a *monogram*. It stands for Louis Vuitton!"

I blink in confusion.

"Louis Vuitton—the famous fashion designer?" Amara cackles.

I stare at her blankly. She looks back at me like I was raised in, well, a stable.

"Ugh, just trust me," she says, jamming a hand smugly on her hip. "This jacket could belong to almost anyone at

Oakwood. But judging by the cut, I'd say it's from *at least* five years ago."

My heart sinks—five years ago is way before Luis started taking lessons at Oakwood.

"Also?" Amara narrows her eyes at me. "Why are you tied to a horse with a bike chain?"

"Don't worry about it," I snap, still not ready to give up on my friendship with Luis.

I turn back to him, my eyes wild with desperation. "But what about the purple pen? You were right next to it when Amara fell during the Halloween parade. It *proves* you wrote me all those secret notes!" I fish the melted remains out of my jacket pocket . . . and twirl the twisted carcass in my fingers.

Amara looks between me and the pen, smirking. "You mean the same purple pens that Georgia keeps in a giant box in the office?"

My mind flashes back to the Oakwood office during the Halloween party, and the box of pens on the cookie table. I remember reaching up to hand one to Gray so I could check his handwriting—I could have sworn the ink was blue. But now I can't be sure . . . it was dark and I was under a table next to a disembodied head.

"I didn't realize those pens were purple," I say softly.

Blergh, I'm such a fool. *Everyone* who's ever set foot (or hoof) in Oakwood probably owns a purple pen.

Which means that anybody could have written the notes.

Which means I just mortified myself in front of Luis in a way that no one has ever mortified themselves in the history of history. Blergh × infinity!

"Sorry, Wills." Luis shrugs. "But I didn't write you all those notes."

"Of course you didn't," I whisper, staring down at my boots and wishing I could disappear inside them.

"Nope, Luis definitely did *not* write you all those notes," Gwyneth says, bounding into Clyde's stall and dragging Everleigh, Noel, and Gray along.

"*Pfffffftttttttttt!*" Clyde snorts happily. He seems thrilled that the entire Oakwood Flyers team has set up camp in his stall to watch my epic mortification. I, however, keep my eyes pointed firmly at the ground, my cheeks burning as hot as the center of the sun.

"Because we *all* wrote them!" Gwyneth continues, her voice soaring.

I look up, startled. I am now drenched with stress sweat, chained to a horse, and epically confused.

"We took turns!?" Everleigh explains excitedly. "We had to use our opposite hands to disguise our handwriting? Like if we were right-handed, we used our left hand, and if we were left-handed—"

"I think she gets it," Amara interrupts her, smiling gently.

"We were really sneaky!?" Noel gushes.

"Yeah," Gray snorts. "We kept writing clues to throw you off—it was hilarious."

 222

"I wrote the one that said 'adore' so you'd think it was Gwynnie?" confesses Everleigh.

Noel tugs my sleeve, looking concerned. "I wrote the one about Clyde being hurt? We were all really worried about him . . . and you?"

"Luis and I wrote that 'don't lose your head' one!" Gray laughs, interrupting Noel to high-five his partner in crime. "Mostly so I'd have an excuse to throw a bloody head at him."

I giggle in appreciation.

"The last clue about the Valiant place? That was all me," Gwyneth says proudly. "I think Clyde's stall is by far the most valiant place I know! But I'm sorry it made you think all the notes were from Luis."

"Well, I *could* have written all the notes," Luis insists, pretending to be offended. "I just wanted to give everybody else a chance, too."

I smile back at him sheepishly.

"Wills, we just wanted to make you feel welcome here," Gwyneth continues. "Secret notes are kind of an Oakwood tradition."

Amara lets out a huff. "Well, nobody told *me* you were writing her notes. And I'm the team captain!"

"We, um, didn't want to distract you from your captain duties?" Everleigh says tentatively as the other Flyers hold their breaths.

But the answer seems to satisfy Amara. "I *do* have a lot on my plate," she sniffs.

Luis kicks some dirt on the stable floor with his boot, then grins at me. "Sorry I had to play dumb about the notes before, Wills."

"Me too?" Everleigh adds earnestly.

"We promised each other we wouldn't tell you until after the invitational, when we were all together?" Noel explains.

Before I can respond, Georgia bursts into Clyde's stall. "Well, there you all are—I was about to file a missing person's report for an entire equestrian team!"

"Sorry, Georgia," Gwyneth says. "We were just . . . solving a mystery."

"Whoa, whoa, whoa!" Georgia says, hustling toward me. "What in the *heck* is going on here?"

I glance down and remember that I am still locked to a horse. Which means I have no choice. I muster my courage, straighten my shoulders, and reveal my top secret plan.

"I chained myself to Clyde," I declare, lifting my chin defiantly. "This way you can never put him up for auction."

"With *my* bike lock?" Kay asks, sticking her head in the stall. (Oh great, exactly who I need to join the party.)

"Kay, this is an act of protest—just like the suffragettes!" I explain. "It was in one of the trivia questions you were studying for Knowledge Maestros."

"The suffragettes didn't steal their sisters' bike locks!" she says indignantly.

"Well, they *would* have. If they were trying to save their best friends!"

Then I turn back to Georgia. "If you're going to send Clyde away from his home, then you'll have to send me, too. He and I are locked together—forever."

Georgia lets out a low whistle. "Wow, kiddo. I appreciate your spunk. And your moxie. And your love for Clyde. But you know this isn't going to work, right?"

She zaps me with an *I'm serious, young lady* look. "Now go on and unlock yourself."

My eyes plead with her, but she shakes her head and kicks the dirt. After a moment, I let out a defeated sigh, then reluctantly dig my hand into my jacket pocket to fish out the key.

"Thank you," Georgia says, reaching for it. But instead of passing it to her, I flick the key over my shoulder into the tall pile of hay just outside Clyde's stall.

"Oops!" I say, pretending to be as surprised by my own strength. "It must have slipped. I guess Clyde and I will have to stay together now!"

Everyone in the stall stares at the pile of hay in stunned silence. Except for Kay. Who promptly strides over to Clyde, sneezes three times, and jostles the bike lock. It magically springs open.

"Kay! What are you doing?!" I cry as the cable slack spirals into a loose pile at my feet. "How could you?"

"You don't need the key if you know the combination," she says. "By the way, you're going to have to buy me a new bike lock now that this one's been contaminated with *horse*."

 225

She sneezes three more times to make her point, before softening her voice. "Wills, you know you can't stay chained to a horse for the rest of your life, right?"

And that's when I realize—*for real* this time—that the jig is up. My months of stupid hoping and wishing and plotting to save Clyde have all been for nothing.

"I'm so sorry, boy," I say softly, throwing my arms around him and burying my face in his chest.

"Pffffffttttttttt," he sighs, nuzzling my head.

I don't care if Luis Valdez and Gray Dawson and Amara and the triplets and Georgia and Kay—if everyone in the entire stable—is watching. I begin to sob uncontrollably—my shoulders heaving and my face slick with salty tears (and snot).

"I did everything I could," I blubber. "I joined the team, I practiced so hard, I jumped clean, I came up with *several* genius rescue missions . . . but I still let you down, boy."

As my chest heaves, I feel a sea of arms enveloping me. Georgia, Gwyneth, Everleigh, Noel, Gray, Luis—and even Kay—all wrap their hands in a giant hug around me and Clyde. Even Amara reaches out from a few steps away to gingerly pat my shoulder.

"We tried really hard?" Noel whispers.

"Noel, we weren't supposed to say anything?" Everleigh scolds her sister.

"What?" I sniffle.

"We tried to raise the money to save Clyde ourselves,"

Luis says in his rumbly voice.

"Yeah, we set up this Go-Pay-Me crowdfunding thing," Gray adds.

"It was Gwynnie's idea?" Noel explains. "And Georgia helped us!"

"We took all these supercute photos of Clyde and posted them so people would, like, donate money to keep him at Oakwood?" Everleigh explains.

"That's what we were doing the day you saw us in the tack room," adds Noel.

Gwyneth's smile falters. "But in the end, we only raised half the money we need for his stall fees. We're really sorry, Wills—we're the ones who let you down."

I look slowly around the room. "You did all that for me and Clyde?"

They nod and hug me tighter as I melt into a mush of feelings. But after a moment, Gwyneth lifts her head and tilts it to the side.

"Wills?" she says with surprise. "I think there's one more note."

I glance up and follow her gaze to the back corner of Clyde's stall.

"Guys," I sniffle, my arms still wrapped around Clyde. "I appreciate it, I really do. But I'm not in the mood for more silly notes right now."

"But we didn't put it there!" Gwyneth insists, her forehead crumpled in confusion. "I swear."

I look around, my eyes questioning each of them, but the Flyers all shake their heads in innocence.

"Enough!" I say sharply. "I'm losing my best friend. We all tried to save him, and we all failed. And there's nothing a stupid note can do to fix it."

"Hey now," Georgia says gently, "what's that old saying? Don't look a note horse in the mouth?"

"Aren't you going to go see what it says?" Gray asks.

"You could at least take a peek?" Everleigh adds.

"If you don't, I will!" Luis threatens.

"Fine," I grumble, realizing it's the only way they'll all leave me alone. I untangle myself from Clyde, then drag myself over to the corner of his stall. I tug down the note, which has been tacked to one of the wooden slats. Big surprise: It's got a purple ⟲ on the front, just like all the others.

"I know you're all trying to make me feel better," I sigh. "But it's pointless."

"Open it!" Noel whispers bossily.

"Okay, okay!" I say, unfolding the note and reading it aloud.

> Dear W,
>
> You won Clyde's heart
> When you walked through these doors.
> There's no need for tears,
> The big guy's all yours.
>
> —A friend

I rub my eyes and blink, then reread the whole thing.

The big guy's all yours.

Brrrrring.

Georgia looks down to her phone. "Well. Look at this—we just got another donation on Go-Pay-Me."

"How much?" Gwyneth asks nervously.

Georgia lets out another low whistle. "Let's just say Clyde is never going to worry about his boarding fees . . . *ever* again."

I flip my head toward Georgia, stunned.

"Seriously?" Everleigh asks.

"Seriously," Georgia says as the rest of the Oakwood Flyers let out whoops of celebration. "It looks like our fine Mr. Clyde Lee now has an official home here at Oakwood.

"You know . . ." Georgia glances at me above the hubbub. "I've been thinking that Clyde Lee would make a very fine mascot for the stable." She pauses to stroke his mane. "That is, if you'll be in charge of caring for him, Willa?"

I must be in shock because I try to say something— *anything*—but no words come out. I nod frantically instead.

"Is that a yes?" She grins.

"Yes!" I squeal. "Georgia, how can I ever thank you? I've never been this happy in my entire life!"

"It's not me you should be thanking," Georgia says, nodding behind me. I turn around and follow her gaze to . . . Amara?

She's leaning against a stall rail. And clicking a purple pen.

"What?" Amara says innocently. "I couldn't be the *only* one who didn't write you a secret note, could I? That wouldn't be very becoming of a team captain."

"But I thought you said—"

"You and Clyde are now both *permanent* members of the Oakwood Flyers," Amara replies, cutting me off. "And the Oakwood Flyers take care of one another."

I open my mouth to speak, but I'm once again too stunned to form words.

"Besides"—Amara smiles archly—"I got my mom to pay for everything. I told her if she didn't, I'd quit show jumping altogether."

My heart practically explodes. "Thank you, Amara!" I yelp, rushing over and tackling her in a bear hug.

"Eeek—you're dripping purple sweat?" she says, wriggling out of my embrace.

I wipe my eyes on my jacket sleeve and smile gratefully at her. Then I run over to Clyde and plant a sweaty lavender kiss on his nose. "Together forever, boy?"

"Pffffffft!" he agrees, stamping a medium-pizza hoof to make it official.

I glance around the stall at Georgia and the other Flyers. "Thank you—all of you. I guess I was so afraid I'd never make any human friends that I didn't realize how many I already had."

"Enough! I can't take any more!" Kay blurts, frantically wiping her eyes.

"Are you crying?" I ask her under my breath.

"Of *course* not," she sniffs. "My horse allergies are obviously getting worse. So I, uh, better go wait in the car. See you there, Wills. And . . . you know, good job today. Go team!"

She hustles away before she has to process any more "allergies."

As the Oakwood Flyers gather around our new mascot, Clyde, and (finally) pose for our team photo, I think about all that's happened since I became an official #HorseGirl.

It turns out that you *do* have to be ready for surprises in life—the happy kind, the sad kind, and even the annoying-big-sister kind. Your parents can't always be there to cheer you on, even if they wish they could. Your ~~secret~~ A friend crush doesn't always ~~secret~~ A friend crush back. Your favorite horse in the whole world sometimes falls down . . . and sometimes so do you. But your friends—even the least expected ones, even the ones you *thought* were out to get you, and *especially* the ones with four legs—will be there to help pick you up. If only you'll let them.

Click.

CHAPTER FORTY

Swoooooosh.

Mom's smiling face glides onto my phone screen. I can't wait to tell her every single thing that just happened.

"Moooooooom!" I nearly burst as I walk down the stable aisle, FaceTiming her. "You are *not* going to believe the story I'm about to tell you."

"Ooh, Willa, hang . . . think . . . have . . . bad . . . connection." The sound cuts in and out as her face freezes.

But as I look more closely at the frozen screen, I notice something odd. There's a handful of people in the background, waving from behind my mom—one of whom looks a lot like . . . Kay? And that guy definitely looks like . . . Dad? And that car sure looks like . . . *it's in the Oakwood parking lot?*

"MOM?" I shriek, running as fast as my feet will carry me outside. "You're home!"

ACKNOWLEDGMENTS

This book exists only because of the endless generosity of my sister, Lindsay Seim—the original #HorseGirl. Lindsay shared with me her exquisite, hilarious, and heartbreaking memories of learning to jump on a gentle giant named Clyde Lee. This story is as much hers as mine. Thank you, Lindsay, for riding lead in my forever herd.

Thank you to author-whisperer Karl Jones for your unbridled enthusiasm, your gentle guidance, and your giant leap of faith. To my ride-or-die Brian Clark for insisting I say yes, for answering my dark-night-of-the-soul calls, for sharing your genius. To my beloved champions, The Crays, for opening your home, your hearts, and the whole world to me. My dear Clarké, what would I do without your steady wit and careful eye? Everything is better since you jumped into my life.

I'm indebted to the brilliant Penguin Workshop team

(especially Nathaniel Tabachnik, who galloped in to save the day) for giving me a go at my first rodeo. To my agent Merrilee Heifetz, I'm honored and thrilled to have you at the reins.

Many thanks to two gifted veterinarians—Dr. Lueen Mansfield and Dr. Sarah Adams—for sharing your expertise and horse love. Thank you to the entire whip-smart Adams family (especially Paige, Colin, and Tristan) for graciously welcoming me into your herd.

To my stable of writer and editor pals who champion and challenge me: Shweta Jha, Heather Alexander, Pat Miller, Trent Preszler (who built the canoe that started it all!), David Cashion, Ayman Mohyeldin, Brandon T. Snider, Margi Conklin, Nathan Burstein, Emma Sloley, Adam McCulloch, Mark Ellwood, Molly Graeve, Rob Muraskin, Gloria Pitagorsky, Tina Anderson, and David Kaufman.

Above all, thank you to my parents, Don and Sharon Seim, who let me go to horse camp even though I was really, *really* allergic. Who read to me every night of my childhood. Who've read (and reread and proofread) every word I've written with unwavering delight. *How deep is the ocean, how high is the sky?*

But some animals . . . leave a trail of glory behind them.
They give their spirit to the place where they have lived,
and remain forever a part of the rocks and streams
and the wind and sky.

—Marguerite Henry